C0-CFH-981

"It's all right," Greg murmured over and over.

He held her tight, kissing her tear-stained face.

The words didn't matter. It was the touch of his lips, the feel of his beard against her skin, the scent of him, that counted. He was tenderness, compassion, understanding. He was life.

The tears and heartache faded, replaced by a hunger to taste the pleasures he was promising. Gentleness was not a necessity. To be taken, to be loved—those were the feelings Amy longed to experience.

Common sense was gone. Reason had vanished. She kissed him back with need and desperate yearning. Life was too short, too quickly crushed out.

And she didn't want to die never knowing the love of a man.

Dear Reader,

Warning! Don't read April's terrific lineup of Silhouette Romance titles *unless* you're ready to catch spring fever!

The FABULOUS FATHERS series continues with Suzanne Carey's *Dad Galahad*. Ned Balfour, the story's hero, is all a modern knight should be—and *more*. Ned gallantly marries pregnant Jenny McClain to give her child a name. But he never expects the powerful emotions that come with being a father. *And* Jenny's husband.

Garrett Scott, the hero of *Who's That Baby?* by Kristin Morgan, is a father with a mysterious past. He's a man on the run, determined to protect his daughter. Then Garrett meets Whitney Arceneaux, a woman whose warmth and beauty tempt him to share his secret—and his heart.

Laurie Paige's popular ALL-AMERICAN SWEETHEARTS trilogy concludes this month with a passionate battle of wills in *Victoria's Conquest*. Jason Broderick fell in love with Victoria Broderick years ago—the day she married his late cousin. Now that Victoria is free and needs help, Jason will give her just about anything she wants. Anything *but* his love.

Rounding out the list, there's the sparkling, romantic mix-up of Patricia Ellis's *Sorry, Wrong Number* and Maris Soule's delightful and moving love story, *Lyon's Pride*. One of your favorite authors, Marie Ferrarella blends just the right touch of heartfelt emotion, warmth and humor in *The Right Man*.

In the coming months, look for more books by your favorite authors, including Diana Palmer, Elizabeth August, Phyllis Halldorson and many more.

Happy reading from all of us at Silhouette!

Anne Canadeo
Senior Editor

LYON'S PRIDE
Maris Soule

Silhouette ROMANCE™
Published by Silhouette Books New York
America's Publisher of Contemporary Romance

If you purchased this book without a cover you should be aware
that this book is stolen property. It was reported as "unsold and
destroyed" to the publisher, and neither the author nor the
publisher has received any payment for this "stripped book."

A special thanks to: Dr. Joseph Alberding;
Kat Adams; Janice McNearney; Kim Fritz; and the
Kellogg Community College library

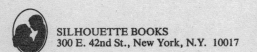

SILHOUETTE BOOKS
300 E. 42nd St., New York, N.Y. 10017

LYON'S PRIDE

Copyright © 1993 by Maris Soule

All rights reserved. Except for use in any review, the reproduction
or utilization of this work in whole or in part in any form by any
electronic, mechanical or other means, now known or hereafter
invented, including xerography, photocopying and recording, or in
any information storage or retrieval system, is forbidden without
the permission of the publisher, Silhouette Books, 300 E. 42nd St.,
New York, N.Y. 10017

ISBN: 0-373-08930-9

First Silhouette Books printing April 1993

All the characters in this book have no existence outside the
imagination of the author and have no relation whatsoever to
anyone bearing the same name or names. They are not even
distantly inspired by any individual known or unknown to the
author, and all incidents are pure invention.

®: Trademark used under license and registered in the United
States Patent and Trademark Office and in other countries.

Printed in the U.S.A.

Books by Maris Soule

Silhouette Romance

Missy's Proposition #864
Lyon's Pride #930

MARIS SOULE

was born in California but now lives in Michigan with her husband and family. The author of numerous category romances, she is now happy to be trying her hand at the Silhouette Romance line. Maris believes that marriage takes a lot of commitment and energy, but it's the best thing that can happen to a person. When Maris and her husband married, they decided to take one year at a time, renewing their ''unwritten'' contract each May. So far they've renewed it 23 times—not bad in this day and age!

Leo says: A wise lion sees what others pass by.

Chapter One

The emergency buzzer from the clinic sounded, jerking Amy Fraser's attention away from the television set. Quickly she uncurled herself from the couch and slipped on her shoes. The television was still on when she limped down the hallway toward the back door that connected the house to the clinic. It was such a miserable night out, that the buzzer could mean anything. The Barnetts' baby's cough might have gotten worse. Mr. Wilcroft might have come by for more arthritis medicine for his wife. Or there might have been a car accident.

Rainy nights always made her think of that.

Again the buzzer sounded, its ragged, nerve-jarring call resounding through the empty clinic. "I'm coming," Amy yelled ahead.

A gust of cold air hit her the moment she opened the door, cutting through her gray sweatshirt and blue jeans. Standing under the eaves, clearly illuminated by the outside light, was Mel Freeman, the old handyman who lived in the small apartment above the general store.

He nodded, then spoke, his southern Hoosier dialect twangy. "Evenin', Doc Amy, I got me a feller out in my truck that don't look t'good. Found him by th' side of th' road. I think maybe he's gone and broke his leg."

Amy looked beyond the handyman, past the plywood fund-drive thermometer on the lawn, to the battered black truck parked in front of the clinic. She could see the form of a man sitting on the passenger's side, his shoulders hunched forward and his head lowered.

"Want f'r me to bring him in?" Mel asked, and Amy's gaze came back to him.

She knew Mel was strong and healthy, but she wasn't about to ask a man in his seventies to single-handedly bring an injured man inside. "I'll give you a hand."

"No need," he insisted. "I can manage."

She ignored him, along with the rain and the cold, and started down the walkway. "Anyone I know?"

"I hain't never seen him 'round here." Mel answered, and matched his steps to her awkward gait. "Said his name's Greg. Greg somethin' er other. Can't hardly understand the feller, he's a shiverin' so much. Found him lyin' by th' side of th' road, huddled 'neath a sleepin' bag. Nearly didn't see him and might not have if he hadn't started wavin' his arms."

A strong gust of wind hit, pelting them with icy rain, and the old man moved closer to block Amy from the storm. "Y'shoulda put on a coat."

He was right. His yellow slicker was keeping him dry and warm, while she was rapidly getting wet and cold. But she hadn't wanted to take the time to get her raincoat. If she had, she knew that Mel would have brought in the man by himself. It was Mel's nature, the nature of most of the people who lived in the area. They were independent, self-reliant and sometimes downright stubborn.

She also hadn't realized how really bad it was out. Wasn't April supposed to bring the showers, and May the flowers? It was crazy. Just the week before, the temperature had been in the high seventies. Now it was storming, the fragrant pinks and alyssum that bordered her sidewalk were about to be washed away and snow wasn't out of the question.

The streetlight created an eerie halo in the inky darkness, and within its circle raindrops turned into shimmering gems. Every step brought her closer to Mel's truck, and she could now clearly see the man inside. He sat huddled over, his eyes closed. From what she could see, he had high cheekbones, a well-defined forehead and a broad nose. He also had very wet, tawny-blond curls that hung halfway down his back, a scruffy beard and a mustache that almost hid his mouth.

Long hair and beards weren't that common around Wyngate, and Mel had said he didn't know his passenger. Amy knew she'd certainly never seen Greg what's his name before. His was not a face she would easily forget.

A skittering tingle coursed through her body, and she shivered, goose bumps rising on her skin.

"You're not gonna like th' way he smells," Mel yelled over the wind. "And he's soaked clear through t' his skin. Even th' sleepin' bag he was under's all wet. I just tossed it in th' back."

The way the rain was coming down, it wouldn't take long for anything to get soaked, herself included, Amy realized. "Where exactly did you find him?"

"Ov'r near Proctor's corner, this side of Miss Emily's place."

Amy knew the spot. After three years of living and practicing medicine in southern Indiana, she was used to how directions were given. No streets or roads. Locations were designated by the names of people or long-remembered and oft-told incidents. It was certainly different from the way directions were given in Chicago, and it had taken her forever to get around when she'd first arrived.

Mel opened the truck door, giving her an even clearer view of the man inside. Immediately Amy smelled pig and wrinkled her nose. The odor had to be coming from the burnt sienna-colored mud that covered the man. It was all over his faded and torn down-filled jacket and on his ragged, khaki shorts, and the one high-topped hiking sneaker he wore—which was practically in shreds—was caked with it. His other foot was bare and also covered with mud, his ankle badly swollen.

Hunched forward, he'd wrapped his arms across his chest. He was wisely trying to hold in whatever warmth he could, but with little success. His teeth were chattering and wherever there was a bare spot, goose bumps covered his legs.

When she looked back up, she found him staring at her, his blue eyes dilated and glazed with pain. If he noticed the scars on her face, nothing in his expression showed it. Shivers racked his body, and she put aside the idea of splinting his ankle. It was more important to get this man inside and warm.

Lightly she touched a clean spot on his thigh. His skin felt cold, but there was a firmness to the muscle beneath her fingertips, a tautness akin to a coiled spring. She hoped it meant he had some strength left. "Greg, can you help us get you out of there?"

He nodded and gritted his teeth, using both hands to move his right leg, then swinging his left leg around so he was sitting sideways on the seat.

"I'll get y'feller," Mel said and moved closer. "Just put your arm around my shoulders and lean on me, like y'done before. Doc Amy, here, will have y'feelin' better in no time. Won't y' Doc?"

"I'll sure try," Amy said, moving to the injured man's other side. "Put your arm around me, too. Whatever you do, Greg, don't step on that foot."

He mumbled an answer that she assumed was agreement, and Mel took one side, she the other. She slipped her arm around Greg's waist, and felt the shivering of his entire body. Although he wasn't a tall man, probably no more than five-ten or eleven, his shoulders were a good three inches above hers. Snuggling close to his side, Amy ignored the smell of pig and tried to transfer some of her warmth to his body.

Keeping the injured ankle immobile was important, but that was no easy feat when every step she took was uneven. As they slowly moved toward the clinic, she could hear Greg's quick intakes of pained breath and knew the distance must seem unending. Even for her, with the rain soaking her clothes and the icy wind cutting through her body, the path from Mel's truck to the clinic—past the six-foot-high plywood thermometer with its painted red indicator, that was slowly rising with each contribution offered to maintain a clinic in Wyngate—seemed unending. The moment they were inside and the door closed behind, all three of them sighed in relief.

"Let's get him into the X-ray room," she directed Mel.

It was the largest room in the clinic, yet always seemed cramped because of the gargantuan antiquated X-ray machine that sat beside the table in the center. She knew the machine had to look like a scary monster to children, which was why she'd hung poster-sized copies of comic strips all over the walls and ceiling. A comic strip distracted and amused, and an amused child relaxed, giving her the opportunity to take the X rays she needed.

The theory also worked on adults, and from the looks of his ankle, the man leaning on her shoulder was going to need some amusing.

"We've got to get you up on the table," she told him, and glanced at Mel for help. "On the count of three?"

Mel nodded, and as soon as they had the man between them in position, Amy started counting. "One...two... three."

On three, she lifted.

And Mel lifted.

What she hadn't planned on was receiving help from their long-haired roadside vagabond. At exactly the count of three, Greg reached back, grabbed the edge of the table and pushed himself up.

The balance of power was not equal. Mel's lift along with Greg's push sent the stranger teetering precariously toward her. Instinctively and protectively, Amy's arms went up to stop him from falling. Using her body she pushed back, her hands clinging to his wet, muddy jacket. His chin touched the side of her face, his beard damp but softer than she'd expected, the warmth of his breath streaming through the bangs that fell across her forehead.

He let go of the edge of the table and reached out to her, his fingers digging into her arm. Using her for balance, he pushed himself away, even as she pushed him away. And then Mel pulled, and it was all right. The man between them was firmly stabilized on the table, though his quick intake of breath said it had not been a painless move.

"Sorry if...I hurt...your arm," he apologized, his eyes expressing his concern through his staccato words.

"No problem," she assured him, but there was a problem.

For one brief moment, the fraction of time she'd held him and he'd held her that second she felt his body against hers and his breath on her skin she would have sworn her insides had turned upside down.

Not a very sound medical diagnosis, she knew, but it did describe how she'd felt. What she needed was an explanation as to why she'd felt anything. She didn't even know the man.

With an exhausted sigh, Greg lay back and closed his eyes, and Amy tried to resume a professional manner. Not easy with a patient smelling like a pigsty. Ignoring the odor as best she could, she quickly checked his pulse, studied his vital signs and analyzed his overall condition.

There were abrasions on both of his knees, he was covered with mud and his skin was cold and abnormally pale. She had no idea how long he'd been out in the rain before Mel found him, but the man was thoroughly chilled. The first thing she needed to do was get him out of his smelly, wet clothing. That alone would help bring up his body temperature and make them all more comfortable. She unzipped his jacket.

Immediately his eyes opened, and he stared at her.

She was dazzled by how blue those eyes were. How intense. "I need to get your clothes off," she explained. "We need to get you warmed up."

He shivered and nodded, his teeth continuing to chatter. "Freez . . . ing," he managed to get out.

She pulled one sleeve loose from his arm. "How long have you been out in this rain?"

"Since . . . it . . . started."

That would have been around six o'clock. For four long hours the man in front of her had lain out on the wet and cold ground, protected by no more than a nylon sleeping bag. Mel helped lift Greg, and Amy slid the other sleeve free, pulled the muddy jacket away, and tossed it into a far corner.

Next came his T-shirt. It was also wet...and covered with mud. Mel might have found Greg under a sleeping bag, but the man had been wearing only his T-shirt and shorts when the storm hit. "What did you do, crawl through a pigsty?"

she asked, tossing the smelly shirt into the corner with his jacket.

"I think he musta crawled through Miss Emily's pumpkin patch," Mel supplied. "Years ago she kept pigs there. Once that smell's in th' ground y'never get rid of it."

"Was...cutting 'cross...country," Greg stammered. "Tripped over a branch...and twisted my ankle...coming down a hill."

She was pretty sure he'd done more than twisted his ankle. Once she examined it, she'd know. His shorts needed to come off, but they were going to take more work than his jacket and T-shirt. Getting him warm was of primary importance.

Amy gave Mel a towel and told him to rub the worst of the mud off Greg's arms, but not to touch his legs. Not yet. Then she limped out of the room. First she turned up the heat, then she exchanged her smelly, wet sweatshirt for a dry one and finally, from the clinic's hall closet, she pulled out two wool blankets.

Greg managed a weak smile and a feeble thank you when she covered him with both blankets. Mel's rubdown had brought some color back to the man's skin, and the warm air blowing into the room would help. It was time to examine his injuries.

She touched his swollen right foot, and he gasped and swore under his breath. The look he shot her was hostile.

"I'm afraid this is going to hurt a little," she apologized.

Maybe the grunt he made was agreement. Maybe it wasn't. She didn't bother to ask. A quick examination, and she was certain the ankle was broken. Badly broken.

Which gave her two choices. She could splint him, call an ambulance and send him to one of the hospitals in Bedford, or she could take X rays right now, see how bad the break was and then decide if she could reduce the fracture herself. Her X-ray machine was old and cumbersome, but considering the physical condition of the man in front of her and how much pain he was in, she didn't think he needed to be moved again and subjected to a thirty-mile trip before getting relief.

Going out to her reception desk, she picked up a patient admittance form and attached it to a clipboard. Pen and clipboard in hand, she came back into the room. Greg was cocooned under the blankets, and Mel was chatting away, talking about the cartoons on the ceiling. "I've always liked that one," he said, pointing up. "And I use t'like *Lyon's Pride.*"

Mel's hand moved to point out the next enlarged cartoon strip tacked to the ceiling, but as Amy neared the table, he glanced her way. "Kinda surprised y'got that one up."

She understood what he meant. "I still love the old ones."

"That there comic strip's been real nasty t'ward doctors lately," Mel explained for Greg's sake. "Real nasty."

"I should enlarge some of those nasty ones and use them for dart boards." Amy chuckled. "Seems only fair. If a cartoonist can throw barbs at doctors, doctors should be able to throw barbs at the cartoons." Clipboard raised and pencil in hand, she turned to Greg. "Mel said your name is Greg. Is that right?"

He nodded and glanced around the room. She had a feeling he was seeing it for the first time. Truly seeing it— cartoon strips, old-fashioned X-ray machine, faded wall-paper and all.

"Greg what?" she prodded.

"Ly...man," he said slowly, staring at the *Lyon's Pride* cartoon above his head. "Gregory Lyman...with a *Y.*"

Gregory Lyman. She wrote the name on the form. "Address, Greg?"

"Three..." He stopped, and she looked up from the form. He was still staring at the cartoon strip, lost in thought.

"Three?" she repeated.

He came back to her with a smile. "Three, nothing. I forgot. I no longer have an address."

"No address?"

"I don't live anywhere. No job. No home."

Another statistic of the economy, she realized and drew lines through the spaces for address and phone.

"Once you get my ankle popped back into place and taped up, may I camp out on your lawn?" he asked. "Just for the night, of course."

"You can stay here," she agreed, but he wouldn't be camping on her lawn. Not in this storm, and not with that ankle. It was going to take more than a mere popping back into place and taping, and she had enough beds and bedrooms to accommodate several homeless travelers.

She decided the rest of the personal data could wait. A man who described himself as having no job probably had no health insurance, either. At least she had his name, and from his accent, she'd bet he was at least originally from the New York area. How he got to southern Indiana or why he was in Wyngate, she'd find out later. Her first priority was his ankle. "Are you allergic to any medication?"

"Medication?" Once again a wary look of distrust invaded his eyes. "Why?"

"I want to give you a shot for pain."

"No," he said firmly. "No shots. No pills. I don't want anything."

"I think your ankle is broken, not just sprained." She had a feeling that information would change his mind. "If so, either I'm going to have to realign those bones or send you to Bedford."

Mel mumbled his agreement with her diagnosis. Greg didn't concur. "It's not broken. I can move my foot."

He did, but a quick intake of his breath expressed his pain, and Amy saw his fingers tighten on the edge of the examining table. She didn't think she needed to say anything more.

Again he surprised her.

"No shots," he repeated through clenched teeth. "Just do what you've got to do."

"Greg, I don't want to give you anything you don't want, but reducing a fracture can be very delicate work. I can't have you all tensed up and screaming every time I touch you."

"I won't scream," he insisted.

He might not want to, but she knew what he'd be going through. Hers had been a broken hip, fractured jaw and crushed facial bones; his was an ankle. She'd been ten; she guessed he was in his thirties. Nevertheless, pain was pain.

"No." She shook her head and turned away, heading for her phone. "I think the best thing for me to do is call for an ambulance and send you over to a hospital in Bedford."

"No, don't do that," he said with an urgency that stopped her. Once again she faced him.

"Whatever you do, don't send me to a hospital."

"You'd get better care there," she insisted. "Look at what I've got for an X-ray machine." Every time she looked at it, she remembered the state-of-the-art machines she'd taken for granted while doing her internship. "Any day it's going to quit on me."

"No hospital," he resolutely repeated, then softened the demand. "Please."

She felt stupid for not understanding. Gregory Lyman didn't have a home or a job. He didn't think he could afford to go to a hospital. "They'll take care of you, no matter what you can pay."

"Oh, I'm sure they'll take care of me." Pure sarcasm laced his words. "I will not go to a hospital. Either you fix this ankle, or splint it and let me find someone who will fix it."

His attitude irked her, and she was half tempted to splint his leg and send him on his way. But only half tempted. Pain made a lot of people say irrational things, and it was her job to help him. Slowly she limped back toward him. "All right, no hospital. But if you need surgery, I can't do it here. I just don't have the help or equipment. If those bones need to be pinned, I *will* splint you and send you on your way. Do you understand?"

"I understand." His answer was clear and unequivocal.

"And what do you suggest we do to keep you from climbing the wall the moment I touch your ankle?"

"I don't know. I just don't want any pills or shots." Greg anxiously watched her near his foot. He might talk and sound brave, but his eyes relayed fear.

"Want me t'hold him down?" Mel asked.

"We'll see." Actually, she didn't think they would reach that point. Given time, she was pretty sure Greg would change his mind. So, she would give him time. "First I need to get him cleaned up."

"I do smell like a pig, don't I?" Greg wrinkled his nose while he kept a close watch of her, every muscle taut. "I was halfway down a hill when I stepped on that limb. The rain had already made the ground slippery. Next thing I knew, I was rolling head over heels. That's when I heard my ankle pop and felt the pain."

"So, how'd y'get to th' road?" Mel asked.

"Crawled." Eyes as wary as a cornered cat's stayed on Amy. "I thought once I reached the road, someone would find me, but after a while, I began to think no one used it."

"Not t'many go t'see Miss Emily," Mel said, "but every Tuesday she fixes me supper, and I tend t'what needs tendin'."

A small smile touched the older man's mouth, and Amy wondered just what of Miss Emily's needed tending every Tuesday night. She pushed the blanket up to the bottom of Greg's shorts. He tensed. "You're not going to sneak in a shot, are you?"

"No, I'm not going to sneak in a shot." She held up two fingers for him to see. "Scouts' honor. Just checking your legs. Other than scraped knees, I don't see any problems."

Trying not to get her hands muddy, but failing, she pulled off the one shoe he wore. Next came his sock. Both smelled as bad as the rest of him. They joined the growing pile of clothes in the corner. Grinning, she looked back at Greg. "The shorts have to go, too."

"My shorts?" His eyebrows rose.

"Yes. Then after I get your ankle taken care of, I'll wash your things."

"Laundry services as well as medical. Now, I've heard it all." He studied her face, and she knew this time he was truly looking at her, seeing the uneven bridge of her nose, the reconstructed cheekbones and the scars. With some people, when they looked at her, she saw pity in their eyes. Suspicion better described the look in Greg's eyes. Finally he shook his head. "You don't need to wash my clothes. I've got more shorts and T-shirts. At least I think I do." Greg glanced Mel's way. "My pack still in the back of your truck?"

"Dag-gone it, I f'rgot all about it. That and your sleepin' bag." Mel started for the door. "Must be gettin' addled in my old age. I'll go get it 'fore it's soaked clean through."

Greg watched Mel leave and sighed. "I should have set up camp when I first saw that storm front."

Amy moved from the end of the table to his side. "Have you been living in a tent for long?"

"Since the end of March."

"That's a long time." She patted the section of blanket covering his hips. "I still want those shorts off."

"Oh yeah?" He grinned rakishly. "You saying you want me to take off my pants?"

Something in his tone made her heart skip a beat, but she ignored it. The only flirting men did with her was in a teasing, playful way. She'd learned a long time ago not to take it seriously, to counter with teasing of her own. "That's what I want."

"And do you always personally undress your patients, Doctor?"

"Only when they're turning blue, and my nurse has gone home for the night." Not that he was blue anymore.

Still watching her, he reached under the blankets. From the movement of the material, she guessed he was unbuttoning his shorts, then she heard the sound of a zipper. She smiled at his modesty. After four years of medical school, two years of internship and three years of practice, she'd seen too many men without their clothes on to count. She was nearly thirty years old. No trembling virgin.

Well, maybe she was still a virgin, though she hated to admit that. And there was a strange, trembling sensation in the pit of her stomach and a warm glow in her cheeks, which she couldn't explain. She glanced at his face and found him watching her.

"Are you blushing?" he asked.

"Of course not," she lied. "Why would I blush? I'm not the one undressing under a blanket."

"It is kind of silly, isn't it," he admitted. Still watching her, he pushed back the blankets, exposing his shorts.

They were unbuttoned, the zipper down, and Amy could clearly see a V-section of silky, black nylon. She hadn't ex-

pected him to be wearing a pair of skintight briefs. Nor had
she expected the trembling, skittish sensation in her stomach to turn into a full-fledged gastric attack. Or her skin to
be feverishly hot. In the blink of an eyelid, she'd lost her
professional distance. Quickly she looked up at the ceiling,
her gaze catching the *Lyon's Pride* cartoon. Leo the lion was
doing cartwheels. The message in the balloon above the
lion's head was simple: "If thrown for a loop, just land on
your feet."

Maybe she didn't like what Leo had been saying for the
last year or so, but this was good advice. What she needed
to do was land on her feet, get control of the situation.
Taking a calming breath, she looked back at Greg. "Can
you get your shorts off by yourself, or do you need help?"

"I can do it," he insisted and began to pull and wiggle at
the same time.

But he didn't get very far. With a gasp of pain, Greg
stopped, his shorts still solidly around his hips. "My ankle," he groaned through clenched teeth. "Moved it. Damn!
Give me a minute."

Beads of perspiration formed on his forehead, and Amy
patted his leg. "Let's try another way. Roll to your side."

Without argument, he did as she'd asked, rolling away
from her, over onto his left side and good ankle. His body
was tensed, and she automatically began to massage his
shoulders and back. Slowly she worked her hands over rock-
hard muscles, down toward his hips. He said nothing, but
she could feel him relax. Finally she knew she could move
his leg without putting him in agony and began to work his
shorts down over his right hip. Inch by inch, she exposed
more of his black, nylon bikini briefs. The man definitely
had sexy taste in underwear. . . .

She hated herself for what she kept thinking, yet the
wayward thoughts continued to slip into her head. Lightly
she brushed her fingertips over his hip. She told herself it

was to make certain his briefs weren't wet, nothing more. She found the material only slightly damp and wasn't sure if she was pleased or disappointed. She could leave his underwear on.

"Now roll over to your other side," she ordered.

He obeyed, slowly and carefully rolling toward her.

As she pulled down on his khaki shorts, she tried to keep her gaze on the pale hairs that covered his legs and not let her eyes stray to the bulge beneath the silky-smooth, black nylon. She wasn't successful.

What she saw surprised her. Considering the cold and the pain he was in, an arousal was the last thing he should have had.

Her gaze darted to his eyes, and once again she found him looking at her, directly at her face . . . at her scars.

Thinking what? she wondered. *Being aroused by what?*

Certainly not her. She was too realistic to imagine that.

Chapter Two

Gregory groaned inwardly. What was happening to him? Were forty-seven days on the road turning his brain to jelly? He shouldn't have gotten lost that morning, or slipped down that hill. And he certainly shouldn't be having these feelings now.

Not for a doctor.

Not him.

Maybe as well as hurting his ankle, he'd bumped his head when he took that tumble. A slight concussion might explain why a woman's hands on his back had turned him on and why the more she tugged at his shorts, the more he was getting aroused. If he were honest, he would have to admit that it had started even earlier, when he'd nearly fallen off the table. He could still remember how she'd felt when he grabbed her, her arms so small yet supportive. How he'd wanted to hold on to her.

It had to be a bump on the head.

Reaching up, he touched his scalp, carefully feeling for a tender spot.

"You all right?" she asked, her voice slightly husky before she cleared her throat. "Does your head hurt?"

"Just checking."

He felt nothing. No bumps. No tender spots. Simply wet, matted hair.

Something crazy was going on. Otherwise, how could he explain the way he was feeling? The woman standing beside him certainly wasn't beautiful, not with those scars on her face. And other than telling him to take off his shorts, she hadn't said a damn thing that could be called provocative. Hell, she wasn't even dressed provocatively.

Maybe her jeans, still wet from the time she'd been outside, did cling to her legs a little, showing off very nice thighs and calves, but her hips were completely covered by the baggy sweatshirt she wore. And the sweatshirt she had on now was even less flattering than the one she'd had on earlier. At least with that one being wet, he'd gotten a hint of a full, firm bustline.

She moved away from his legs and quickly examined his head, her fingers probing where his had just touched. Then she checked his eyes. "Look at me," she ordered, and he did.

He looked deep into a sea of green, and saw concern. That or she sure could fake a worried expression.

"Now look to the side," she said.

He obeyed and hoped she didn't see too much in his eyes. Didn't recognize his face.

"Your pupils look fine, and I couldn't feel any bumps. Do you remember hitting your head?"

"No." He'd simply been searching for an excuse, a reason why he found her attractive. Dammit all, she was a doctor. His enemy. Only, for some reason, he didn't see her as the enemy. Not this woman.

She moved back to his hips and resumed tugging on his shorts. Head bent, she kept her gaze on his legs, not higher, and like honey, her chin-length hair spilled forward. She didn't have the curl he had. Actually, her hair had very little curl. His mother had always hated his curls, always made him cut them off. So did the army. One year after his discharge, he had curls to his shoulders. Now they were halfway down his back.

"I'm going to pull your shorts off the rest of the way now," Amy warned and slowly began to work the wet and muddy material down his legs.

Her tone was professional, but she sounded tense. As tense as he felt. Closing his eyes, he waited for the pain.

The touch of her hands was a warm caress against his skin. She was trying to be gentle, moving slowly, first working his good leg free. Next, and just as carefully, she began working his shorts closer to his swollen ankle. Greg didn't look, but listened, hearing her take in a breath and hold it.

The room had an antiseptic smell and he smelled like pig, yet he could also smell her. She had a scent about her that made him think of sunshine and flowers. He'd noticed it when they were outside in the rain, when she'd first put her arm around him and helped bear his weight. He hadn't wanted to lean on her then, not as dirty as he was and not with her limp, but she'd held him securely, and he'd been too cold to object. Too cold and in too much pain.

He was warm now, and if he kept his right leg very still, it didn't hurt.

Her knuckles grazed his ankle, and pain instantly shot up his leg. Thoughts of sunshine and flowers vanished. Clenching his fists, he wondered how he could make it through this ordeal without something to block the pain.

He wanted to think he could. It had been sixteen years since he'd taken anything stronger than aspirin. Sixteen years of freedom, of clear thinking and the energy to live life. He didn't want a reminder of how it had been before.

"I'm going to wash the mud off your legs," Amy said, and he opened his eyes. "It may hurt, but I have to do it. We can't have any dirt on your skin if I have to put your ankle in a cast."

"Okay," he said and waited tensely, mentally trying to prepare himself for the pain. She took her time, filling a bowl with water and getting a washcloth and towels. When she came back, she smiled reassuringly. He tried to smile in response.

He could imagine how he looked, scratched up and dirty, his long hair matted. Probably like a wet cat. No, the way he smelled, more like something the cat dragged in.

Greg was ready for her to start with his bad ankle and was surprised by the slightly rough feel of a warm, wet cloth on his left leg. Lying flat, he couldn't see exactly what she was doing, but he could feel. Her touch was gentle, each stroke cleansing his skin and stimulating his circulation. "This should make you feel better," she crooned softly.

If she wanted him to relax, she was succeeding. She was also getting him just a little excited, especially when she moved her hand and the cloth up between his legs. He tried to stop it, but he could feel his body responding.

And he knew the moment she noticed.

Suddenly her hand stopped moving, and she looked up, her gaze meeting his. Then quickly she looked down, a flush of color tingeing her cheeks. Next she moved the cloth to the outside of his leg. He saw her bite her lower lip, and he grinned. Doc Amy was embarrassed. A woman who should be immune to this kind of thing, was blushing. He found it endearing.

When she had his thighs cleaned, she covered him down to that point with the blankets. "Dag-gone, it's gettin' worse by th' minute," Mel called out, the outside door slamming closed behind him. "Thought I'd better see if I was gettin' any water in my tool box, but just checkin' got everythin' wet. Then I really had a mess."

The old man came into the room carrying a large, muddy gold backpack in one hand and a blue nylon sleeping bag in the other. He glanced at Amy, then at the wet, muddy pack. "Got a rag I can use t'wipe this thing off?"

"Go ahead and take a rag and towel from the hall closet," she answered. "Second shelf."

Mel went back out into the hallway, and Amy finished her job. Greg watched her face. When she reached his ankle, she took no pleasure in his pain. If anything, he'd swear that every time he flinched, she flinched. Every time he held his breath, she held hers. And when she was finished and he sighed, she also sighed, then looked up at him. "I'll get a couple of X rays, then we can see what needs to be done."

He could tell she was trying not to move his ankle any more than necessary, but after one set of X rays, he was in a cold sweat. When she showed him the pictures, even he could tell his ankle was broken.

"It's bad, but not as bad as I'd feared," she said. "It doesn't need to be pinned. I should be able to do it myself. That is, if that's what you want. I can still call an ambulance and get you to a hospital."

"No." He hadn't changed his mind about that, but the idea of her pulling on his foot to put those cracked and misaligned bones back into place sent a chill down his spine. Maybe he didn't want his head all fuzzy, but he also didn't want to start screaming like a wild man. As she studied the X rays, he gave in. "Okay, you win, give me something."

She looked his way. "Something?"

"For the pain. I guess I'm not as tough as I thought."

She smiled smugly. "You're not allergic to anything?"

"Nothing I'm aware of." And he'd certainly had enough medicine dumped down him when he was growing up to have found out. The only reaction he'd ever had was to fall asleep.

She prepared the shot and gave it to him. It didn't take long before he began to feel the effects. Looking back, the events of the day seemed a lot funnier than they had earlier. "I must have looked like a bowling ball going down that hill. Where the hell did these hills come from, anyway? Yesterday I could see for miles in every direction. Today I decide to cut through a few fields, and bang, I'm looking at a twenty foot drop."

Mel nodded. "Farther south you go, the hillier it gets, too."

"You're getting into the Uplands," Amy explained. "The glaciers didn't make it this far. Just a few miles from here, there's a ski resort."

Greg eyed her suspiciously. "Are you pulling my leg?"

She tugged on his ankle. "I guess you could say I am, but no, I'm not kidding."

"Miss Emily calls this God's country," Mel said proudly. "Some folks think we're behind the times, but that's not so. We jest know what we need and what we don't need." He nodded toward Amy. "Doc Amy here is one thing we need, and we aim to keep her."

Greg didn't understand.

She explained. "The hospital that was funding this clinic has run into a financial bind. I've been cut out of the budget."

"But we don't want her leavin'," Mel insisted. "We like her, and she understands us. So we're gonna raise th' money t'keep her here."

Greg heard the affection in the old man's voice and saw it in his eyes. Doc Amy had a loyal follower.

She stopped pulling on his ankle. "That should do it. How are you feeling? Any pain?"

"No pain at all." Whatever she'd put in that shot was better than anything his mother had ever given him. "I'm ready to kick up my heels and go dancing."

She laughed at the idea. "Before you do, let me get one more X ray and that ankle in a cast."

"A cast might hamper my dancing." And his cross-country walk. Not that he cared at the moment.

Amy adjusted the X-ray machine. "Dancing may be out for a while, but a cast is going to make your leg feel a whole lot better and will keep those bones from shifting position. Don't move now." She nodded at Mel. "Time for us to step out of the room again."

She seemed pleased with the second X ray. Ironically, Greg was willing to take her word that everything was in place. The way he felt, she could have turned his foot around backward, and he wouldn't have cared.

Mel yawned, and Amy glanced at her watch. "It's getting late, Mel. Why don't you go on home and get some sleep?"

"Whatcha going t'do with him when y're done?" he asked, nodding toward Greg.

"Keep him here, at least for the night."

"Think that's safe?"

She smiled. "He's not going to cause any trouble."

"Well then, won't y'need me around t'get him t'a room and t'bed?"

Amy shook her head. "I'm sure Greg and I can manage. You go ahead and go home. And thanks for bringing him in."

"Yeah, thanks," Greg said. His face felt flushed, and he knew he was smiling foolishly, but he couldn't seem to help it.

"No problem, feller." Mel gave him a warning look. "You treat Doc Amy good now, y'hear. She's our sweetheart."

Greg watched Amy's cheeks turn pink. Not a bright pink, but just a hint that accentuated the narrow white lines that marred her face. "I'll treat her like my sister," he promised.

Like my sister. After Mel left, Greg wondered why he'd said that. He didn't even have a sister, and the way he'd been feeling earlier had definitely not been brotherly.

Lying on his back, watching Amy wrap his swollen ankle with a thick, protective padding, he wondered about his reaction to her. Being stuck in a doctor's office in Nowheresville should have him nervous as hell. Instead, she made him feel safe. Protected.

It was strange.

Amy glanced up and caught him looking at her. "So, tell me about yourself," she said.

He wasn't sure how much information to share. "What do you want to know?"

"Where you're from?"

He'd tell her that. "New York."

"City or state?"

"City."

She smiled and limped over to a cabinet. "I'd guessed as much. You're a long way from home. Why'd you decide to come to Indiana?"

"I'm walking from New York to California. Southern Indiana's along my route."

Her glance was quick. "That's a lot of miles to walk."

"I know."

"And when you get to California?"

"I decide what I'm going to do with the rest of my life."

"That's quite a goal." She came back with a package that she began to tear open. "And you couldn't make that decision in New York?"

"Maybe, but I wanted to get out and see the country, talk to people."

Amy glanced down at his ankle. "You're not going to be doing any walking for a while. Not without crutches, at least."

"So how long will I need crutches?"

"The way that break is, I'd say three weeks before you put any weight on that ankle. After that, you should be able to use a walking cast."

Three weeks on crutches. Even as relaxed and happy as he felt, that didn't sound good.

As she wrapped the cast around the padding, he watched her. One thing he'd already learned, she licked her lips whenever she was concentrating. She also kept glancing his way, her concern for how he was doing evident. She'd been concerned about Mel, too. Greg didn't want to like Doc Amy, but he did. He didn't want to be attracted to her, but he was.

Again she ran the tip of her tongue over her lips, and he found himself wondering what it would be like to run *his* tongue over her lips. What she would do if he kissed her? He had a feeling that wasn't the way a man should think about a woman he'd just promised to treat like a sister.

Amy looked up and caught him staring at her. Immediately she looked down again, then slowly back up. "If you're wondering about my scars," she said, "I was in an accident when I was a child. It was a night like tonight. Raining hard. A drunk ran head-on into the car my aunt was driving, and I wasn't wearing a seat belt and went through the windshield."

Greg cringed at the thought. "Is that why you limp, too?"

She nodded. "The doctors could fix my hip, but they couldn't make that leg grow like the other one."

"I'm sorry." He truly was. For the pain she must have gone through, and for making her think he was staring at her scars. "I hardly noticed your scars."

She scoffed. "They're a little hard to miss."

"It was your mouth I was looking at."

"My mouth?" She stared at him for a moment, then frowned. "Why were you looking at my mouth?"

"I was wondering what you'd do if I kissed you."

Amy laughed, shook her head and went back to work on his cast. "That shot I gave you must have put you in La-La Land."

Maybe she was right. He normally didn't go around telling women he barely knew that he wanted to kiss them. He certainly never thought he'd say it to a doctor.

But she did have tempting lips. "Are you married?"

She didn't look up. "No."

"Engaged? Have a boyfriend?"

"No, and sort of?"

She did glance his way, and he raised his eyebrows. "Sort of?"

"There's a stone carver here in Wyngate I occasionally date. I wouldn't actually call him a boyfriend."

"Meaning you go out with him, but you don't love him?"

"Meaning we occasionally go out. We're friends. That's all." She gave the cast a final check, then looked up. "Why all the questions about my love life?"

To be honest, he didn't know; yet he was glad there wasn't another man in her life. He gave a slight shrug. "Just curious. Something to talk about, I guess."

She began to clean up. "What about you, then? Are you married? Engaged? Have a girlfriend?"

"Not married and not involved with anyone. I was engaged once, but it didn't work out." He grinned foolishly. "She didn't think I took life seriously enough. She said I was a kid who'd never grown up. Said—"

He stopped himself. Another minute and he was going to tell her his life story. That would be cute.

And foolish.

He stared up at the enlarged comic strips on her ceiling. "I've never heard of anyone hanging cartoons on the ceiling."

"It keeps the patients amused. Especially the children." She shot him a quick glance. "You probably didn't notice when we brought you in, but the walls of my waiting room are covered with cartoons. I needed new wallpaper, but couldn't afford any, so wherever I had a hole or a spot, I covered it with a cartoon from the newspaper. After a while, my patients began bringing them in for me to put up. Now one wall and part of another are completely covered. Instead of reading magazines, my patients read the walls."

It was an interesting idea. "You even put up *Lyon's Pride* cartoons?"

"I've got a lot of the old ones up."

"But none of the ones from the last year or so?"

"A few." She faced him and leaned back against the counter as she dried her hands. "Hey, if I can laugh at blonde jokes, I guess I can laugh at doctor jokes, too."

"Some doctors don't like them."

"I can understand why. To be honest, I haven't found any of his recent ones the least bit funny. It's like he's out to do a hatchet job on doctors." Her expression turned serious. "I sure wouldn't want to be in his position."

"Why's that?"

"Well, let's say Mr. G. M. Lyon needs a doctor. After all the lampooning he's done on doctors, what do you think might happen to him?" Amy chuckled and tossed her towel with the others she'd used on him. "All kinds of possibilities come to mind, don't they? How's your ankle feel?"

Greg tensed. "My ankle?"

"Is that cast getting hot?"

He could feel heat radiating through the padding to his ankle and leg. Warily he looked at the cast, then back at her. "It's warm."

"That shouldn't last too long. It's just a chemical reaction. Nice thing about modern medicine. By the time I get your knees cleaned up, that cast will be set. Which, of course, means I can get you to bed faster."

He knew she didn't mean it the way it sounded, and under normal circumstances he would have let it slide, but these weren't normal circumstances. The warmth coming from his cast was normal. His ankle was going to be fine. That knowledge combined with the effects of the shot she'd given him left him unable to resist teasing her. "Now that's the best offer I've had in a long time."

"I mean—"

She stopped, her cheeks once again turning pink. Then she grinned. "Sorry, buster, a bed is all you're getting."

"Do you always put your patients up for the night?"

"Whenever I want to keep an eye on them."

"Ah-ha, so you admit it, you want to keep an eye on me." He pushed himself to a sitting position, and immediately regretted the move. Objects went out of focus, walls swayed, and one doctor became two. Greg gripped the edge of the table, his own body swaying.

Amy hurried to his side, grabbing his arm. "You all right?"

Her voice soothed, while her fingers provided an anchor. He stared at her. "It depends. Is the room going 'round in circles for you?"

"No." She placed her other hand against his forehead.

Her palm felt cool and soft. He put his hand over hers, holding it there. "Nice," he murmured. "Very nice."

"You'd better lie back down," she suggested.

"No, I'm fine." The room was no longer spinning. Focusing on her eyes was helping. She had such beautiful eyes. A sea of green. A man could get lost at sea.

He was lost.

Chapter Three

"Lie down," Amy ordered, careful to support his neck and shoulders as she gently pushed back.

Greg resisted, rigidly remaining upright. "No."

"If you feel dizzy, you need to lower your head." His pupils were dilated, and the way he kept staring at her, deep into her eyes, made her uncomfortable. She moved her hand out from under his and away from his forehead.

"I'm fine," he said firmly and looked away. "Where exactly am I, anyway?"

"Where?"

"What town?"

She gave up trying to get him to lie down. "Wyngate, Indiana. Population fourteen hundred, give or take a few." It would probably be take. "We're located about ninety miles south of Indianapolis and around forty miles north of the Kentucky border."

Greg sighed wearily. "A guy I met this morning said there were some interesting limestone grave markers I should see, so when I saw a sign for a cemetery, I decided to take a side trip. I thought I was headed in the right direction, but I sure didn't end up where I expected. How'd you get here?''

"How'd I get here?"

"You're not from this area originally. You don't talk like these people."

"Not everyone around her says, 'Y'know livin' in Wyngate's not f'r everyone from Chicago.' "

"You're from Chicago, then?"

"A suburb. My folks and sister still live there."

"You moved from Chicago to a town of less than two thousand?'' His laugh was incredulous. "Why?"

"Because I like it here."

"What about the money? Certainly a Chicago doctor makes a lot more money than a Wyngate doctor."

"Money's not important to me."

"Sure. And what if I tell you I can't pay you?"

She'd suspected as much. "No problem."

"No problem? What is this place, a subsidized charity ward?''

"Not subsidized. At least it won't be after July first. And I have been trying to get my patients to keep their accounts paid up. On the other hand—'' which the comptroller from the hospital hadn't understood "—I will not turn away people who need my help just because they don't have the money to pay me. I took an oath to heal sickness, not to check bank accounts."

In that case, she was unique. At least from his experiences. "And what happens after July first?"

She sighed. "The hospital will no longer be subsidizing this clinic. Actually, it's more than money. They don't like some of the things I do."

Greg smiled knowingly. "Like what?"

"Like they think I spend too much time on each patient, that I need to be more efficient. That I shouldn't make house calls, that I—"

"You make house calls?" he interrupted.

"Yes."

"A doctor in this day and age who makes house calls." He laughed, shaking his head, his mane brushing across his bare shoulders. "I think I am in La-La Land."

Amy stiffened perceptively, her mouth becoming a tight line. "Maybe you and the hospital comptroller think it's a stupid idea, but the people around Wyngate like it. That's why they've started this drive to raise enough money to keep me here. They also bring me food. Help me around my house. I don't need to make a lot of money."

"Then you're one in a million."

"No, I'm not," she protested. "I know a lot of doctors who care about their patients first and money second. We can't help it if malpractice insurance costs an arm and a leg. Or the equipment we need to make an accurate diagnosis comes with six-figure price tags."

"Or that your membership in the country club, your yacht and your mansion all take money."

He was upsetting her now. "Mister, even if I wanted to join a country club, I wouldn't have the time to enjoy it. And a yacht would be silly on any of the lakes around here. Of course, my mansion does have many rooms, but I don't think you're going to find it very fancy."

He said absolutely nothing, but she could see the change in his eyes. From a hard, smoldering blue they grew softer and warmer. Finally he smiled. "I guess you are different."

"I'm just me. Scars, limp and idealism."

The idealist meets the cynic. He shook his head at the irony.

Greg remained sitting up. It gave him a sense of some control, and she kept close watch of him as she treated his knees. More than once she paused to look into his eyes, check his pulse and ask if he felt dizzy. He supposed she was worried about him going into shock or passing out. He knew his eyes weren't exactly focused and that he grinned a lot, but that he blamed on the painkiller she'd used. He also wanted to blame that shot for the warmth flowing through him every time she touched him, for his soaring pulse rate when her fingers grazed his bare thigh and for his growing fascination with her.

The more he stared at her, the more he tried to decide what it was about her that appealed to him. He still wouldn't call her beautiful, but the scars on her face seemed less significant now, and in spite of her limp, she did have an innate gracefulness. She was also much stronger than she looked—setting an ankle wasn't easy.

She had very pretty hair, its myriad shades of honey-blond creating a soft frame for those big green eyes of hers. And her nose, though not perfectly straight, was as small and delicate as the rest of her. It was her mouth his gaze kept coming back to, her lips so full and lush. She was chewing on her lower lip, concentrating on his knees, then she looked up and smiled, and he knew analyzing her face, feature by feature, would never explain her appeal. It was an inner glow she projected. A feeling.

Without questioning why, he grinned back.

"That should take care of your knees," she said, straightening and brushing her hair back from her face. "I'm not going to bandage them. Will you be all right if I leave you alone for a few minutes?"

"Of course," he said, only he didn't want her to leave. Maybe he'd been alone too many nights. Or maybe he just wanted her to keep talking to him, touching him, looking at him with those lovely sea-green eyes and smiling at him with that lush, full mouth.

She left, and in spite of the massive X-ray machine, the room seemed empty. He sighed, unsure of his feelings, and leaned forward to touch the cast that encased his right leg from his toes to below his knee. It was no longer radiating heat and was surprisingly hard.

What was he going to do now? His decision to take off and walk to California had been impulsive from the beginning, driven by anger, not logic. Sore muscles and blisters had been his first clue that he should have planned better—conditioned his body. He'd gotten past those problems, but now this? Considering how he'd been going through the hiking sneakers he'd been buying, even if he had a walking cast, he doubted it would last very long.

He couldn't even rent a car and drive. Not until he did have a walking cast, and maybe not even then. Besides, a car would get him from point to point, but it wouldn't give him the chance to talk to people. Not the way he'd been doing for the last forty-seven days.

Brian had said he needed to stop fighting a personal vendetta and get on with his life. "You need to take some time off and smell the flowers."

Greg doubted Brian had expected him to put his things in storage and one week later walk away from it all. But that's what he'd done. Literally walked away and started smelling the flowers.

He sniffed the air.

The smell of a doctor's office was one he'd known from as far back as he could remember. Knew and hated. But there was another aroma in this room. He sniffed again, then grinned. She'd asked if he'd crawled through a pigsty. Well, her X-ray room now smelled like one. No wonder she'd wanted his clothes off.

Glancing up at the ceiling, he stared at the lion in the *Lyon's Pride* cartoon. "Did you see me earlier, Leo? Didn't think I'd ever get aroused by a doctor taking my clothes off.

Of course, I've never had a woman doctor take my clothes off before.''

The lion said nothing, but that didn't stop Greg from going on. ''She's different, Leo. And you know what's crazy? I kind of like her.''

When Mel had stopped and picked him up, the old handyman had said that he would like Doc Amy, that she'd fix him up good. Soaked to the skin, freezing and in more pain than he'd ever experienced in his thirty-four years, Greg hadn't objected. Nevertheless, he hadn't expected to like any doctor. Hadn't expected to end up in a small town clinic, being treated by a doctor who blushed.

He definitely hadn't expected to be attracted to her.

But he was.

''So what do you think?'' he asked the lion above him. ''What do I do next?''

''We get you to bed and you get some sleep, that's what you do next,'' Amy answered, coming into the room. Over one arm she had draped something large, gold-colored and fluffy. In her other hand she held a pair of aluminum crutches.

Greg warily watched her near the table. The object draped over her arm looked suspiciously like a woman's robe. ''What's that?''

''Something to keep you warm on the way to bed.'' Leaning the crutches against the table, she used both hands to hold up the robe, spreading it open for him to see.

Something warm and decent, he decided. The over-sized robe did look like it would fit, and it would be better than prowling around in his skivvies. But a woman's robe?

''Try it on,'' she urged, holding it toward him.

''I've got a change of clothes in my pack.'' Fluff wasn't his style.

"Do you really want to go through the process of getting dressed just to walk a few feet down a hallway to a bedroom?"

The real question was, did he want her helping him put on his clothes? The answer was yes...and no. The way his body had been reacting, he was better off if she didn't touch him any more than necessary. He studied the robe. "No one's going to see me in that thing, are they?"

"No one," she assured him. "The clinic's connected directly to the house. We'll go down the hallway, through a door, and there's a bedroom just a few feet farther on. You'll have the robe on and off in no time."

She continued to hold it toward him, and he finally took it. The material was as soft as kitten's fur but thick and heavy. It would keep him warm. Chuckling, he slipped it on, pushing the blankets aside as he did. "Good thing Brian can't see me now."

"Brian?" she asked, picking up on the name.

"My—" He stopped himself. Next thing he knew, he really would be telling her his life story. That would be cute. Again, he chuckled. "Brian's a friend. One who's not afraid to tell it like it is. For years we've had a debate about what makes a 'real' man. I think we'd agree on this one. I don't think a *real* man would wear a woman's robe."

Maybe not, but for Amy, Greg's masculine image didn't decrease when he put on her robe. Not one bit. The gold material blended with his long mane of hair and beard, and when he looked at her, his nostrils slightly flared, he reminded her of a lion. A proud, noble lion.

"I want you to take it easy getting off the table," she said, moving close enough to help if needed. "Don't put any weight on your right leg."

He pushed himself forward, wiggling his way to the edge until his left foot touched the floor tiles. Carefully he eased himself down, using the table for balance, then he paused. The color drained from his face, and he weaved.

"Take a deep breath and lower your head," she ordered, bracing him with her body.

"I'm okay," he insisted, his voice shaky. He did take a deep breath, but he kept his head high.

"Don't move until you feel stable." She was beginning to regret sending Mel home. If the man in front of her collapsed, she was going to have a heck of a time getting him to a bed.

Another deep breath and he nodded. "I'm all right. Just give me those crutches and watch me go."

He was stubborn and too full of male pride to admit he was about to collapse. He was going to be a handful, but she liked his gumption. One by one, she handed him the crutches. He slipped them under his armpits, the padded armrests disappearing into the fluffy fibers of the robe. She'd made a calculated guess when she adjusted them, and it looked like she'd guessed right. As soon as he had them in place, he nodded toward the door. "Lead the way."

She wasn't in that big of a hurry. "Ever used crutches before?"

His no triggered a lesson in the basics of walking with crutches. In his case, she showed him the swing-to gait. Once she was sure he understood, she took three steps back, giving him room to move. "Take it slowly."

When he was once again in front of her, she continued to move back, working her way toward the door. Each step he took, she matched, her gait as awkward as his. By the time they reached the hallway, a fine sheen of perspiration covered his face, but he was still on his feet.

"We just have to go down this hallway." She pointed the way.

Greg stared at the door at the end of the hall. It was maybe twenty feet away, no more. After days of walking twenty-five to thirty miles, it should be easy.

It didn't take him long to amend that thought.

Each step of the way she encouraged him, yet by the time they reached the door, he was in a cold sweat and ready to collapse. He wasn't a man who liked leaning on a woman, but he willingly leaned on her when she put her arm around his waist.

"Breathe in deeply through your nose and slowly let it out through your mouth," she ordered. "Do you feel nauseated? Lightheaded?"

"Lightheaded," he admitted. And he didn't like it.

"After I open this door, there's a bedroom just a few feet away. In the morning, when I have patients in the clinic, it won't be as quiet as some of the other bedrooms you could use, but I think close is better than quiet."

He nodded, and as soon as his breathing was normal, she opened the door. Stepping through, she waited for him to follow. "Just a little way more now."

Greg looked into the house. The walls were painted the same white as those of the clinic, and the boxlike construction was basically the same, yet the hallway had an entirely different atmosphere. A feeling of warmth seemed to radiate from the other side of the door. Even the smell was different, the aroma of antiseptic replaced by the sweet scent of flowers. Swinging his crutches forward, then his body, he willingly followed her.

She led him to the first doorway, stepped in and switched on an overhead light. The room was small, with a four-poster double bed, nightstand and antique oak dresser taking up most of the space. Compared to the tent he'd been sleeping in for the last forty-seven days, the room looked immense. All he needed now was a bathroom.

She seemed to read his mind and limped over to a door near the bed. "Bathroom's in here. I imagine you'd like to freshen up before you go to bed."

"Thanks." He swung his way over to the door.

"Can you manage by yourself?"

He wondered what she'd say or do if he said no. Or for that matter, what he'd do. He wasn't ready to find out. "I'll be fine."

Once inside, he closed the door, leaned his crutches against the wall and balanced himself on his good leg. The face reflected in the mirror was pale, and he stared at himself. Wearing the robe, he looked like an oversized, plush toy. A hairy, over-sized plush toy, he decided. Carefully he reached up and touched the shaggy edge of his beard.

Until this trip, he'd never grown a full beard, but he'd quickly learned that shaving while on the road wasn't easy. He'd also decided people would be more willing to talk to him—really open up—if they didn't recognize who he was. The beard could use a trim, however. And so could his hair. Next city he reached, he'd have to find a barber.

Next city. He glanced down at the stark white cast on his right leg. How to get to the next city was going to be a problem.

By the time he came out of the bathroom, he hadn't decided how to manage that feat, but he was cleaner. The soap by the sink was considerably smaller in size, and the towel hanging on the towel bar showed signs of the dirt he'd missed. He'd also used some mouthwash he found in the cabinet. It would have to do until he had the energy to go through his pack and find his toothbrush and toothpaste.

Amy was sitting on the edge of the bed. She'd pulled back the quilted comforter and flowered top sheet and placed an extra pillow down where his right foot would rest. Head bent, eyes closed, she looked totally exhausted, but the moment she heard him, she rose to her feet. "Ready for bed?"

"As ready as I'm going to be." He stopped in front of her. "You look tired."

"I am a little," she admitted. "I turned down your bed and gave you an extra pillow for your leg. You need to keep that ankle elevated for a while to keep the swelling down."

"Yes, Doctor." He chuckled and glanced down at her sweatshirt, blue jeans and sneakers. "You know, even after watching you set my leg and put on this cast, it's difficult for me to think of you as a doctor."

"I do look a little more professional during regular hours. You caught me in my grubs."

He looked back up, and Amy wasn't prepared for the intensity of his gaze. If he was having trouble thinking of her as a doctor, she was failing at thinking of him as a patient. She'd never felt these kinds of vibrations with someone she was doctoring. Such an awareness. So much chemistry.

From the start she'd tried to ignore the feeling, the attraction. She knew she should ignore it now, help him get into bed, say good-night and leave. Instead, she stood where she was, gazing into his eyes . . . hoping he'd kiss her.

Balancing himself on his crutches, Greg reached out and touched her cheek. She tensed as he ran his thumb over a scar. She knew what he was seeing, feeling. Fine white lines ran across her temporal bones and from her nose to her chin. Her face was a map that multiple surgeries had been unable to obliterate.

"Amy." He said her name softly, then hesitated. "May I call you Amy?"

"I don't care." She just didn't want him saying he felt sorry for her, for how she looked. She didn't want his pity.

"I like the name Amy," he said softly. "It's crazy, but I like you, Amy."

His gaze moved to her mouth, and slowly he lowered his head. She knew then that he was going to kiss her, and a small voice inside of her head cried out that she should stop him, that ethically it wasn't right.

Barely breathing, she didn't move.

First the soft, bristly texture of his beard rubbed against her skin, then lips cooled by sweet well water touched hers. Amy could taste the mouthwash he'd used and smell the soap that had washed away the last of the pig odor. His mouth was firm, possessive and demanding, yet his hold was light, and she knew she could pull away if she wanted.

She had no intention of pulling away.

He groaned and cradled her face with his hands, and she felt him sway on his crutches. Reaching out, she grabbed the fluffy fabric that covered his shoulders. A step closer and her body met his, balancing him.

How right kissing this man seemed. Touching. His hands brushed over her hair; hers combed into his, feeling its dampness. He slid his tongue into her mouth, and it was her turn to groan, the sound coming from deep within her, like something trying to escape. What was happening was unreal. Men didn't kiss her, not like this. Men treated her like a buddy, joked and laughed with her about sex, but they never followed through. They made love with their beautiful girlfriends, the ones with the peaches-and-cream unblemished complexions, the ones who walked gracefully by their sides. They made love with women who looked like her sister. The only kisses she ever got were chaste and over too quickly.

This kiss was not chaste, and Greg hadn't ended it.

He held her close, and she moved her hands in small circles over his shoulders and back, feeling the contrast of the softness of her robe to the hard muscles of the man. He brought her hips to his, and there was no doubting the effect she was having on him.

Or the effect he was having on her.

Clinically she knew the words to describe it. But words didn't convey the tingling sensations, the warmth and excitement.

The need.

The insanity.

Suddenly her eyes snapped open. Insanity was the right word. When did she stop thinking rationally and begin acting like an idiot? Here she was, a doctor, kissing a man she didn't even know, getting herself and him aroused. A man who'd told her he'd been on the road since the end of March. On the road alone.

He was still under the influence of the painkiller she'd given him. His mind wasn't clear. He probably didn't even know what he was doing. Tonight she could have looked like Miss Emily, wrinkles and all, and he would have kissed her. It was tomorrow, in the morning, that he would regret his actions.

The thought of what his reaction would be when he woke and the effects of the shot had worn off made her go cold inside. Stiffening in his arms, she pulled back.

He tried to stop her, but that only made her resist with more force. Finally he loosened his hold and looked at her, frowning. "What's the matter?"

"I—" She couldn't tell him her fears, not when the darkness of his blue eyes showed his passion as clearly as his body had. His mind was numbed; he wouldn't understand reason. She had to be the sensible one, the one who put an end to this foolishness. "It's time for me to leave."

"Just like that." He snapped his fingers, but his gaze never left her face.

She felt his mind probing hers, and prayed he couldn't read the confusion in her eyes. It was hell to want something, yet know it was wrong. She couldn't remember a kiss that had ever felt so good. A touch that turned her insides to liquid and made her want so much more. To answer him took all of her willpower. "Just like that. It's late. I have to be up early tomorrow morning."

"Of course." The warmth left his eyes, and he drew into himself. He was taking it personally, like a slap in the face.

"If you'll get into bed, I'll cover you," she offered, trying to soften the blow.

"How sweet. Just like my mommy used to do."

She heard the sarcasm but chose to ignore it. Pulling the quilt and sheet back a little farther, she waited for him to move. "You can lean the crutches against the wall."

He stepped away awkwardly, hopping on one foot while he leaned the crutches against the wall, then he hauled himself and the cast up onto the mattress. He had to twist and wiggle to pull the robe off once he was on the bed. She tried not to look down at his black nylon briefs, yet somehow she could still see them. It was as if her eyes were magnetically drawn to that area of his body.

When he had the robe off, he handed it to her, and she hung it over an end bedpost. "In case you need it during the night," she explained.

He kept watching her, and she hoped he didn't realize how socially inexperienced she was, that dissecting cadavers and examining patients wasn't the same as standing next to a living, breathing, near-naked male who made her blood pressure rise.

Lying back, flat on the bed, he held her to her promise. "Okay, Mommy, cover me up."

Grabbing the edges of the sheet and quilt, she pulled them up, her gaze purposefully skipping over his briefs and all they covered. Someday she would laugh about this. She was sure of that. Someday, but not tonight.

Even though her fingers touched his chest ever so briefly, brushing against the softness of a mat of blond hairs, it was long enough for some unseen spark to jump between them. Electrified, she let go and took a step back.

He watched every movement she made, calling to her even as she retreated. "Aren't you going to kiss me good-night?"

"I think I already did." Forcing herself not to run, she slowly continued her backward progress toward the door.

He grinned. "No, that was our hello kiss."

Hello, and probably by morning, goodbye. She reached the doorway. "If that leg bothers you, or you have any problems sleeping, just yell."

"And if I yell, will you come hold my hand?"

"I'll give you a pill for the pain."

From his frown, she knew that wasn't what he'd wanted to hear.

Chapter Four

A child's screams snapped Greg's eyes open. Then he blinked. Light filtered through drawn shades, illuminating reality. He was in a bedroom, not his tent; in a bed, not his sleeping bag. Confused, he looked around, noticing the cracks in the stucco ceiling, the framed Japanese prints hanging on pastel flowered wallpaper, the antique oak dresser and finally the small alarm clock on the dresser.

Its hands showed it was already past eleven. Eleven in the morning. He'd slept way longer than he usually did.

He pushed back the covers and started to move, then groaned and stopped. Every muscle in his body ached, and his right leg felt unnaturally heavy. Slowly, painfully, he pushed himself to a sitting position and stared down at the pristine white cast that encased his ankle, foot and lower leg.

In a rush, the events of the night before came back. He replayed his memories of Dr. Amy Fraser at a slower speed, trying to remember every tiny detail of how she'd looked, what she'd done and what she'd said.

When he came to the kiss they'd shared, he smiled, then frowned and shook his head. "Way to go, Gregory Michael." Nothing like coming on like an attacking lion.

Actually, he felt more like *he'd* been attacked by a lion. With another groan, he lay back and closed his eyes. How he'd love to go back in time, back to before he saw the storm front and debated whether to cut across that field or make camp. Back to before he had the bright idea of going off his original route to look at limestone grave markers.

The screaming from the other side of the wall subsided to sobs. He remembered Amy had said this room wouldn't be as quiet as others. He held his breath, trying to hear what was being said in the adjacent examining room, hoping to catch the sound of Amy's voice. All he could make out was the child's crying.

Here it was, past eleven, and he was still in bed, while Dr. Amy Fraser was up working. Tending her patients. He wondered what time she'd gotten up. Or how she'd slept.

For hours he'd thought he'd never get to sleep. After she left, he'd lain awake, wondering what he was going to do now that he was on crutches and trying to forget how good it had felt to hold a woman in his arms. Kiss her. Want her.

Not once during those wakeful hours did he consider calling out for something to help him sleep, not even when the effects of the shot wore off and he sobered up from the giddy numbness that had controlled his words and actions.

His entire body had ached, but pain he could understand, could deal with. What he didn't understand was the physical desire he'd felt for Amy. She was a doctor and for the past two years he'd thought of doctors as the enemy. They were money-hungry grubs. An infection that needed to be exposed and cleansed.

Need a prescription? Pay your money and it's yours. More pills? No problem. You have the cash. May as well give you what you asked for. Who would be hurt?

Who cared?

Greg sighed in frustration. Brian had said he needed to get rid of his anger. Sleeping in a doctor's home wasn't helping. It was time to get moving, hit the road.

Again he opened his eyes.

He discovered the good doctor had been in his room since leaving so abruptly the night before. Against the wall near the door, all washed and dried, were his clothes. And next to that stack, were his hiking shoes—if those shreds of leather could still be called shoes; his sleeping bag—dry and in a tight roll; and his backpack—all traces of mud removed. The only item that was missing was his jacket.

On crutches Greg found it difficult to maneuver his pack into the bathroom, but he finally managed. A shower or bath were out, but he proceeded to wash thoroughly, enjoying the feel of hot water, scented soap and a thick, soft towel.

Finally, the dirt washed out of his hair and clean bikini briefs, shorts and a T-shirt on his body, he felt like a new man. He was trimming his beard and mustache when he heard a noise in the bedroom. Opening the bathroom door a crack, he called out, "I'm in here, Amy."

"Well, I'm out here, and I'm not Doc Amy," a sharp, strident woman's voice answered.

Pushing the bathroom door open and balancing on his crutches, Greg turned to face a tall, stocky woman standing by the bed. Indeed she was not Doc Amy. Maybe her mother—or grandmother—though even that seemed unlikely considering the few strands of her hair that were not gray were a dark brown and so were her eyes.

He guessed her to be in her sixties. Perhaps older; perhaps younger. Her skin was wrinkled, but her stance was erect, her voice firm and her gaze piercing. And when she glanced at the soft, fluffy gold robe hanging on the bedpost, then at the unmade bed, and finally back at him, her scowl warned he was in for a tongue-lashing.

"Doc Amy said to let y'sleep in, but I figured noon was long enough." She sniffed and looked him up and down. "I knocked before I came in. Guess y'didn't hear me."

"Guess I didn't." Though he didn't see why not. Her voice was as strong as a street vendor's. "I'm Greg Ly—" He stopped himself, remembering the name he'd given Amy. "Lyman. And you're—?"

"Peggy. Peggy Madison." She studied his hair, then shook her head. "I clean house for Doc Amy. Three times a week." Her gaze darted to the open backpack on the floor in the bathroom. "Y're just passin' through, I take it?"

"On my way to California." He shifted his weight on the crutches.

She looked at the cast on his leg. "'Suppose you'll have to change your plans, now."

"I suppose so."

Again her gaze traveled to his face. "Doc Amy's special. Kindhearted. Generous. 'Round here we think a lot of her."

"So I've gathered." Peggy was the second person in twenty-four hours to tell him how well Amy was liked.

"What I mean is—" she looked back at the unmade bed and robe "—I wouldn't want to think a man took advantage of Doc Amy's generosity. She may not be no beauty with those scars on her face and that limp of hers, but someday she'll make some man very happy."

"I'm sure she will."

Greg moved out of the bathroom, toward the older woman. He was clumsy as an ox on the crutches, but he was learning to get where he wanted to go. It took him less than five seconds to close the space between them. Eye to eye he faced Peggy. "Look, just because Amy's robe is in here, don't go jumping to conclusions. Believe me, last night I was in no condition to take a woman to bed. Any woman."

He leaned toward her, and she instinctively leaned back. "Also, what do you mean, she's no beauty? She may have a few scars and a limp, but she's no ugly duckling."

"I didn't mean she—" Peggy snorted and stepped back. "I've got t'get lunch on th' table. Doc Amy will be through in th' clinic soon. If y'want anything t'eat, be in th' kitchen at twelve-thirty."

She marched out of the room, and Greg stared after her. She was already down the hall before he smiled and murmured, "Thank you, and it was nice meeting you, too."

By twelve-thirty his hair was dry, the snarls all combed out, his backpack was repacked, his bed made and he was ready to give his thanks to his hostess, pay his bill and be on his way... though he didn't yet know what way that would be. He figured, while he had lunch with Amy, he could ask her about taxis and buses. His first step was to find a hotel or motel where he could hole up for a few days, let his body recuperate and decide his next course of action.

In the kitchen, Peggy stood by the sink rinsing dishes. On the table there were two place settings, a bowl of salad, a plate of sandwiches and a white vacuum carafe. Through the windows that faced a large tree-filled backyard, Greg could see it was still raining, the sky a somber, heavy gray.

Inside the kitchen the mood was cheerier, white baskets filled with a variety of indoor plants hanging from the ceiling, the green a contrast to a wallpaper striped in sunshine-warm golds and oranges. And at the end of the counter sat a vase filled with pink and red peonies, their sweet scent filling the room.

Peggy turned to face him and was about to say something when a door opened, then closed, down the hallway behind him. Greg angled back on his crutches and watched Amy limp down the hallway.

Her honey-colored hair bounced with each awkward step she took, her wispy bangs tickling the soft lines of her eyebrows. The night before she'd looked relaxed and casual in her sweatshirt and jeans. Now she did look like a doctor, a white lab coat paired with white slacks and white shoes. Around her neck was a stethoscope, and in her arms she held a grocery sack.

Amy smiled when she saw Greg standing in the doorway to the kitchen. She'd wondered if in the light of day he'd look as good as she remembered from the night before. She wasn't disappointed. Wearing a dark blue T-shirt and navy shorts, the man was absolutely gorgeous, especially his hair. She knew women—her sister in particular—who spent hours in beauty parlors trying to achieve the same soft mass of curls that Greg had been born with. On some men, long hair and curls might have looked feminine, but not this one.

The beard and mustache eliminated any mistaking Greg for a woman, but so did his thick eyebrows, the strong, bold look of his features, and the lean, sinewy muscles of his arms and legs. Always the doctor, she noted the color of his skin was good and the scrapes on his knees looked clean, scabs already forming. Her patient was on the mend.

"'Morning," she said as she approached. "Or should I say, good afternoon? How are you feeling?"

He shrugged. "Like a Mack truck ran over me."

"And your ankle?" She stopped in front of him and glanced down at the cast she'd put on the night before. She could tell his foot was still swollen, but the color in his toes was natural. "Any tingling in your toes? Numbness? Any pain of any kind?"

"My leg feels like it was used as a battering ram, but the pain isn't anything I can't live with. Definitely no tingling or numbness."

"Keep it elevated as much as you can today." She sniffed and grinned. "You certainly smell a lot better than you did last night."

"Thanks to the bar of soap I just about used up." He glanced at the bag she was holding. "Been grocery shopping?"

"This is payment on a bill." Amy glanced beyond him to Peggy. "Eldon Cole brought some asparagus and rhubarb and two dozen eggs. Take a dozen when you leave, Peg, and anything else you can use."

Peggy cleared her throat and looked at Greg, her brown eyes censorious. "I was thinkin' I might stick around this afternoon. At least f'r a while."

Amy frowned. "Why's that?"

Peggy looked away from Greg to Amy. "I wasn't able t'finish th' room *he* was in."

The way the woman said "he," Greg knew she disapproved of him. From the moment they'd met, she'd disapproved. Not that it mattered, he decided. In a short while he would be gone.

If Amy picked up on the animosity, her smile didn't show it. Moving past him, she took the grocery sack to the counter and set it down. "There's no need for you to stay to do that room, Peggy. I'm sure he didn't mess it up that much. You do more than you need as it is."

"And you do more than you need for this town," the woman said firmly. "We all owe you, Doc Amy, and we want t'keep y'here."

"And I appreciate what everyone is doing to keep me here." Amy placed one carton of eggs near Peggy and kept the other for herself. "Take some asparagus and rhubarb, too."

Peggy watched Amy limp toward the refrigerator with her eggs, glanced at Greg, then sighed. Going over to the bag, she pulled out a handful of asparagus spears and several rhubarb stalks.

"So, what's for lunch today?" Amy asked after she'd put her carton of eggs in the refrigerator.

"Salad and sandwiches," Peggy answered.

"I hope you like salads," Amy said to Greg and motioned for him to go to the table. "That or a sandwich is usually all I eat for lunch."

"A salad's fine." He swung his way across the kitchen while Amy washed her hands. As he leaned his crutches against the wall and hopped into position to sit down, he could hear Peggy murmuring something to Amy. A warning he was sure, especially when the woman gave him one last glare before putting on her raincoat, grabbing her umbrella and taking her eggs and vegetables. Amy sat down across from him at the same time Peggy pulled the back door closed behind her.

"She worries too much," Amy said in passing and reached for the white carafe. "Hot tea? It's decaffeinated."

"Sure." Anything hot sounded good. He pushed his cup toward her so she could pour. "I have a feeling Peggy doesn't like me."

Amy laughed lightly, the sound as bubbly as her smile. "She thinks you're a druggy, here from the big city to jump my bones, then steal everything from my medicine supply cabinet."

"And you're not worried that I might be?"

"No." His cup filled, she began pouring tea into hers.

"I did kiss you last night."

He saw her tense, the tea sloshing over the side of her cup. Quickly she put down the carafe and grabbed a napkin. The smile was gone, and not once did she look at him.

He waited as she wiped up the spilled tea, wondering what she would say, expecting her to tell him he'd been way out of line. Instead, when she spoke, her words were hesitant.

"Last night...well...you were...that is..." She paused, bit her lower lip, then took in a deep breath. "It had to have been that shot I gave you."

"I must admit, that shot did make me feel good." He grinned. "Real good."

But it hadn't been the reason he'd kissed her. If it were, why would he still have the urge to lean across the table and kiss those sweet lips?

"Anyway, I'm glad you're feeling better today," she said formally, then pushed the plate of sandwiches his way and began to serve herself some of the salad. Almost absently she added, "Go ahead and put your leg up on a chair."

Obediently he did, all the while noticing she kept avoiding looking directly at him. She was embarrassed by the kiss they'd shared, not angry. Worried he wouldn't have kissed her under normal circumstances. He wished he knew a way to tell her he was also totally confused by this desire to kiss her. What could he blame it on today? The smell of peonies?

"What are your plans now?" she asked.

"To find a place to hole up and lick my wounds. Somewhere where I can decide what I'm going to do next. This town have any taxis? If not, how far to the bus station?"

Amy cocked her head and looked at him. Then she smiled and shook her head. "No taxis in Wyngate. As far as the bus, we do have a stop but no station." She pushed the salad in his direction. "Why leave here?"

"Why?" Her question took him by surprise.

"I have plenty of room in this house." She glanced toward the refrigerator. "I also have plenty of food. I'm in the clinic in the mornings and out on calls in the afternoon, so you'd have plenty of quiet to rest up. Also, if you had any problems with that ankle, you'd have a doctor close by.''

It was a stupid idea. The moment Amy mentioned it, she wished she'd kept her mouth shut. She wasn't even sure what prompted her to suggest he stay, other than she didn't want him to leave.

Was her approaching thirtieth birthday turning her into a desperate old maid? One kiss and she was ready to cling to a man, beg him to stay. She was being ridiculous. That kiss hadn't been because he was attracted to her. He'd been higher than a kite last night, unaccountable for his actions.

But oh how she wished the blue eyes staring at her would lose that wary look. That he'd gaze at her as he had the night before, see her as a woman—a desirable woman. Touch her. Hold her. Kiss her.

Quickly she got her mind off that. "It's still raining outside. Getting anywhere, even to a bus, will be difficult. Especially on crutches and with a backpack."

He had to admit, the idea of leaving this warm, cozy house wasn't all that appealing. His body hurt and getting around on crutches was tiring. Nor—with a cast on his right leg putting him off balance—did he feel that secure on his feet. With his pack on his back and out on wet sidewalks, who knew what might happen? He didn't need to fall again, perhaps break his other ankle.

But to stay with a doctor?

To stay with Amy?

He tried to guess the motivation behind her invitation. Money? Revenge? Did she know who he really was? Had she put two and two together since last night? It was the only thing he could guess. "You figured it out, didn't you?"

"Figured what out?"

"Who I am."

Intently she studied his face, then shook her head. "I'm sorry. *Should* I know who Gregory Lyman is?"

"No . . . no, of course not." Either she was a great actress or her questioning look had meant she really didn't know who he was. That was a relief. It also left money as the motive for her seeming generosity. "Okay, how much is this going to cost me?"

He was confusing her, but Amy was beginning to understand. He was still worried about how much it was going to cost. "My patients pay me in lots of different ways. Eldon Cole sees to it that I'm never out of eggs, and with his garden, I know I'll have fresh vegetables all summer long. Tom Gibson cuts firewood for a living. When his wife had a miscarriage, he paid part of his bill by bringing me wood for my fireplace. And a lot of people in this community have worked on this house." Amy glanced around the kitchen, every wall and window showcasing a variety of skills.

"You ought to have seen this place when I first came here. The clinic had been closed for over three years before the hospital decided to open it again. No one had lived in this house for all that time, and I guess even before then it had gotten pretty run-down. It's been my patients who have made my home a cheerful place to live. They're the ones who papered and painted the walls while I was making calls, sanded down and revarnished the floors and fixed the plumbing. Harry Bozel even built me a gazebo." She pointed to the small, circular, wooden gazebo in her backyard, then looked back at him. "Greg, give whatever you feel you can give. Maybe a few chores around the house when you're up to it."

"Chores?"

"Peggy only comes three times a week and only in the mornings. With me living alone, that's often enough. With another person here, I don't want to give her more work."

"You want me to do chores?" He couldn't believe what she was saying. "And that's all?"

"That's all I'm asking."

"Clean house?"

"Or whatever you do best." Her father had repeatedly told her a man respected what he paid for, and something earned through hard labor, he treasured. Amy believed it. "What kind of work did you do before you lost your job?"

Greg didn't answer right away, and a dozen possibilities popped into her mind. He'd thought she'd recognize his name. With his long hair, he might be a singer. A rock star who'd lost his job with a band and was now headed for California on foot, hoping to succeed there. He could sing for his supper.

She wouldn't mind that.

Or he might be an artist. Artists often had long hair, and she didn't know names of artists.

Heck, he could be anything. A lot of the younger men she saw working on construction projects had long hair and beards. The combination meant nothing, except that certain occupations didn't enter her mind. Bankers—with them it was short hair and business suits. Lawyers—her sister was always telling her lawyers were a conservative lot. Or doctors. Greg's long hair would simply get in a doctor's way.

And he'd definitely expressed an animosity toward doctors, which was all the more reason to keep him around. It was her duty to disprove his cynical perception of her profession as greedy and uncaring.

"I worked in the field of communications," he said finally.

"Communications?"

"I delivered messages." He grinned. "Have any messages you want delivered?"

"Not at the moment." A delivery man hadn't been among her list of probable occupations. For some reason, it still didn't seem right to her.

"Then maybe I'd better find a few things to do around the house."

"Meaning you'll stay?"

He considered the idea, weighing the pros and cons. On the plus side, he wouldn't have to find a motel room, wouldn't have to go out in the rain and would have a chance to see firsthand if Dr. Amy Fraser was as noble and unselfish as she sounded. On the negative side, she asked too many questions. Saw too much with those beautiful sea-green eyes of hers. Was too damned desirable.

He compromised. "I'll stay until the rain stops."

Chapter Five

After lunch, Amy left. Greg couldn't believe she actually did make house calls. Even her explanation about how important it was to see how people lived had sounded unreal. Doctors didn't care how people lived. If they had, his life would have been a helluva lot different, and his mother would probably still be alive.

Long after Amy drove off, leaving him with instructions simply to rest, he sat at the table in the kitchen, staring out the window at the rain, wondering what macabre twist of fate had dropped him into this upside-down world. When he did move, it wasn't with any speed.

Amy had cleared the table, except for his mug and the vacuum carafe. Awkwardly he carried the two items to the sink where she'd stacked the rest of the dishes. Remembering the conditions of his staying, he turned on the hot water. Fifteen minutes later he had their few dishes washed and dried, the sink wiped clean.

He had a feeling Peggy would complain if he left spots.

Amy had said to make himself at home. He did, starting by familiarizing himself with the layout of the house. Off from the kitchen was a combination mudroom/laundry room, one of its two doors the back entrance to the house. Hooks held a variety of jackets, ranging from down-filled to feathery light. On top of the dryer his jacket had been laid out to air-dry. Its colors were faded after forty-seven days and just as many nights of being exposed to the elements, and there was a tear in one sleeve. He remembered snagging it on something while crawling for the road. His fall down that hill hadn't done his clothes any more good than it had his body, and he could imagine Amy's first impression of him—a wet, dirty, smelly alley cat.

And he'd kissed her.

No wonder she said it had to have been the shot she gave him. No rational-thinking man would have dared kiss a woman he'd barely met after coming into her house looking and smelling as he had.

Feeling like a fool, Greg continued his tour of the house. Her "mansion," as she'd called it the night before, hardly equaled the mansions of the doctors he'd investigated.

In Dr. Amy Fraser's mansion, no one decorating or color scheme prevailed, antiques flanked the contemporary and function clearly outweighed beauty. What did prevail was light and color, every room a warm smile on a faded but clean face.

Down the hall there were two bedrooms beside the one he was using—all small but each with a private bath. There was also a formal dining room that looked like it was rarely used, and a living room that appeared to be Amy's entertainment and relaxation center.

Not an inch of space was left open. A television set was flanked by a stereo system, while built into one wall was a huge fireplace and another wall was covered by bookshelves

One large section was devoted to impressive medical tomes, but the rest of her collection surprised him. He hadn't imagined a doctor would have books about folk medicine. At least not books that looked well-read and studied. And her choice of light reading amused him. She had the classics, several mysteries, a few bestsellers from years past and a row of romances.

A doctor who blushed, who stammered out excuses for a kiss and who read romances. He could see why the towns-people wanted to protect her. The lady *was* unreal.

Greg moved past two upholstered easy chairs to the couch. It was large and plush, its beige fabric soft to the touch, its cushions inviting. In front of it was a low, hand-crafted walnut-burl coffee table, the wood polished to a soft gleam. On top lay one book. *The Best of Lyon's Pride.*

Placed there for him to see? he wondered. Or was it simply happenstance? She'd said she liked the cartoon strip— the old ones—and the book's worn cover and dog-eared pages proved it was more than a conversation piece.

From the living room, he could see the staircase that led up to the second floor. He assumed Amy's bedroom was up there, along with more bedrooms and baths. During lunch, she'd explained how the house and clinic had been built by the town's former doctor, the upper floor for his family, the first-floor rooms for patients he wanted to keep overnight for observation.

"The house and clinic came with the job," she'd said. "Though I rarely use the rooms down here. If someone's bad enough to need watching through the night, I usually send him on to one of the hospitals in Bedford. I've never had a man spend the night."

He thought he caught a hint of a blush when she smiled and looked up at him through silky blond lashes.

"Not a man alone."

If it was a blush, she quickly recovered. ''In the last three years, I have had a couple of women stay over who live way out of town and were due to deliver. I wanted them in town in case there were problems. Their husbands stayed, too. Oh, and soon Peggy will be staying here.''

Greg wasn't sure if Amy added that as a warning or simply as an afterthought.

''Just last week she asked if I'd rent her a room. She's having some kind of work done on her house. When she'll be coming, I don't know, but it doesn't matter. She's welcome and so are you. Might as well use the space.''

Maybe Amy didn't care if he and Peggy both stayed, but Greg doubted Peggy would feel the same way. Nevertheless, he would stay. At least until he had more energy.

Simply doing a few dishes and touring the lower level of the house had left him exhausted. Where was the stamina he'd had only yesterday? Where was the energy to walk for miles, up hills and down, under a hot sun or through a pelting rain? He felt like someone had pulled the plug, draining his body of strength. Again he glanced at the soft, plush cushions of the couch. Then with a sigh, he lowered himself onto one.

Almost absently, he thumbed through the book on the coffee table, the familiar panels of cartoon strips barely registering as he glanced at them. It wasn't until he reached the lone picture of a lion that he stopped turning the pages.

''What do you think, old boy, am I making a mistake staying here?''

The lion's smile said it was a joke, and Greg sighed and closed the book. ''So, why did I say I would?''

Because he was tired, he decided. And because a woman with enticing green eyes and a bewitching smile, a doctor who blushed and cared about his welfare, had asked him to stay.

He slipped off his one shoe and lifted his right leg up onto the couch. After he shoved a couple of throw pillows under the cast, he lay back. He'd give himself a few minutes to rest, a chance to recharge. Time to think.

Exhausted, he closed his eyes.

When Greg woke, the sky outside the living-room windows was a smoke-gray, the rain continuing down in a dismal drizzle. The time indicator on the VCR showed it was nearly seven. He'd slept away the afternoon.

Pulling himself to a sitting position, he listened for sounds. He could hear the blower for the gas furnace and the hum of the refrigerator in the kitchen, but otherwise the house was quiet.

Greg got up on his crutches and moved into the hallway. Looking up the staircase, he wondered if Amy had come in, found him sleeping and gone up for a nap herself. As late as she'd been up the night before, she had to be tired. "Amy," he called out.

The house remained silent.

"Amy, are you up there?"

He waited, holding his breath, listening. When there was no answer, he contemplated the stairway. What would have been an easy climb a day and a half ago, now looked monumental. Making a decision, he started up the steps.

By the time he reached the top, his arms and shoulders ached. Looking down the hallway, he tried to decide which room would be Amy's.

It took three tries before he found her bedroom. First he knocked, then he softly called out her name. When she didn't answer, he opened the door. The room she'd chosen for her own was spacious, cheerfully decorated in pinks and yellows, and had a view of the tree-covered hills beyond the town. Her double bed was empty.

But the scent of roses filled the room, and he saw a bouquet in a vase on her dresser, their crimson blossoms beginning to wilt. Roses from the stone carver? Greg wondered. Maybe their relationship was more than just a friendship. That might also explain Amy's retreat the night before, her embarrassment over the kiss they'd shared.

Feeling like an interloper, he quickly backed out of the room and closed the door.

It took him twice as long to get down the stairs as it had to get up, but he realized his long nap that afternoon had helped. He wasn't totally exhausted. Just worried.

In the kitchen the clock said it was now nearly eight. So where was Amy? Stranded out in the rain? In a ditch?

His mind played terrible games. The curse of being creative, he knew. He imagined the worst, then forced himself to consider other possibilities. Perhaps she'd thought about what Peggy had said and while away had given more credence to the woman's warnings. It wouldn't be unreasonable for Amy to have had second thoughts about taking a complete stranger into her house. Maybe she was now staying away, afraid to come home.

A wise decision, he decided. What did she know about him, anyway? His name?

Not really.

What he might do to her?

Even he wasn't sure about that. He certainly hadn't expected to kiss her the night before. Nor to have wanted to kiss her when he saw her at lunchtime.

Peggy could have been right. He could be into drugs. How did Amy know what he might do to her? A leg in a cast didn't mean a man couldn't overpower a woman. Rob her. Make love to her.

Doc Amy was too trusting. That's what she was.

Greg was angry when he heard the back door open. Turning to face the laundry room, he saw Amy before she saw him. "Where have you been?" he demanded.

She looked up, her expression registering surprise, then she continued taking off her raincoat. "Out on calls."

"All this time?"

Amy stepped out of her rain boots, barely giving him a glance. "It took me longer than I'd expected at the Dolfmyers'. How are you feeling?

"Fine." He watched her take off her rain hat and run her fingers through her hair. In soft, honey-shaded layers it flowed to the sides of her face, her bangs dusting her forehead.

Amy limped into the kitchen, her socks feeling a little damp. She didn't want to take the time to take them off. She didn't understand the anger in Greg's tone or the accusation in his questions. The last time she'd had to account to anyone for her whereabouts had been when she'd lived at home, and that had been years ago. "So, what's the matter?" she asked, stopping in front of him.

"What's the matter?" His eyes took on a dangerous glint. "You're out until eight, come home to a complete stranger, and you ask me what's the matter?"

"I'm often out until eight. Sometimes later than that."

"And do you often invite strangers to share your bed?" he demanded.

She stiffened, lifting her chin so she could look him squarely in the eyes. "I did not invite you to share my bed, just my house. Your bed's down here, mine's upstairs."

"I've seen it."

"So?"

"So if I can climb those stairs, what's to keep me from making love to you if I want?"

If he'd been threatening, she might have been worried, but there was too much concern in the question. She laughed. "Come on, Greg, be serious."

She stepped back, so he could look at her. Really look at her. "With this face and my gimpy leg, you're going to want to make love to me?"

Reaching out, he caught her arm in a captive grip. "Don't underestimate your appeal to a man."

Amy tried to laugh, but it came out a squeak. Her heart thudding in her chest and a queasiness in her stomach rapidly approached ulcer stages, she looked straight into eyes of midnight blue and forced herself to sound bolder than she felt. "I am not underestimating anything. I'm being realistic. Men don't find me sexy."

"Is that so? Then explain why I kissed you last night."

"You were in shock. That shot I gave you made you forget reason." The longer she stared into his eyes, the more her voice quavered. "You . . . you weren't responsible for your actions."

"Then why did I want to kiss you earlier today? Why do I want to kiss you right now?"

"You do?"

Maybe she should have been terrified, should have tried to get away, laughed at the idea. Screamed.

She didn't do any of those things.

The only thing she did was lick her lips. . .and look at his.

"Yes, I do." His voice softened, and he drew her toward him. Gently. Slowly.

She stepped forward, meeting him, her hands going to his chest, her fingers curling into the soft cotton of his T-shirt. Through the material she could feel the warmth of his body and the rapid beat of his heart. Tilting her head back, she prayed he wouldn't change his mind.

He sighed as his lips settled over hers, then he groaned. His mouth moved hungrily, with the intensity of a man long-

starved for a kiss. He gave and she took, then returned, her
need greater.

She wanted to remember this moment, hold on to it forever. On a conscious level she registered the soft, rasping
sensation of his mustache and beard against her skin, the
firmness of his mouth and the pleasant taste of him. She
inhaled his manly smell and recognized the scent of her favorite soap and a herbal shampoo. Through her fingertips
she could feel the increase in his heartbeat, the rise and fall
of his chest with each breath he took. She wasn't sure if she
was breathing at all. Didn't care.

This was the way kissing was described in the books she
read, the way she'd always dreamed of kissing a man. No
quick peck, friendly brush of the lips or stiff, obligatory
contact. Greg's fingers were moving over her back, up into
her hair. He was holding her to him, demanding more.

And she gave, her own hands traveling around to his
sides. His tongue probed, and she opened to him. Closer she
inched, the buttons of her white lab coat rubbing against his
T-shirt, her breasts straining to be released from the silky
material of her bra.

He was the lion, and she was his captive. His hold was
deceptively gentle, yet escape was impossible, the ending
predestined. It was a fantasy come true.

She felt his roar of anguish rather than heard it. Jerking
his head back, Greg released his hold on her. His breathing
uneven, he stepped away, nearly losing his balance on the
crutches. His eyes were still dark with passion, but his look
held confusion. "I don't know what . . ."

He stopped, but Amy understood. Years of rejections
made the answer clear to her. He hadn't meant to kiss her.
Not like that. The man had been on the road too long.
Alone too long. She'd been available and had practically
thrown herself at him.

Only he'd suddenly come to his senses.

"I shouldn't have done that," he apologized.

Hurt more than she had been in years, she abruptly turned away. "You're right, you shouldn't have."

"I don't usually come on to a woman like that."

"I understand." Yet it made her want to cry. To scream. Why did he have to come along and show her how it felt to be kissed with passion? Make her want what she would never have? It wasn't fair.

"We'll chalk it up to..." She didn't know what to chalk it up to.

Hormones? Greg wondered. *Abstinence?*

Maybe. At least in part. Yet he knew it was more than that. He stared at Amy's back, her shoulders slumped forward. She should be angry. She looked whipped. "I'm sorry," he murmured.

"No problem." She took a deep breath, her back straightening, then she walked away. "So, have you eaten?"

"No." He watched her move across the kitchen, her steps uneven. She didn't look back at him. "I'm afraid I haven't done much today except sleep. I only woke up awhile ago."

Woke up irritable and aroused, she realized. Just her bad luck to come home while he was still feeling that way. "As Leo says," she stated, heading for the refrigerator, "a long nap deserves a good meal."

"Leo?" Greg questioned.

"Leo the lion." Amy glanced his way. "From *Lyon's Pride.*"

"Ah, Leo." He moved closer. "And how did Leo get into this conversation?"

"I don't know. I guess maybe you remind me of a lion." She fluffed her fingers through her own hair. "You know, a lion's mane?"

At his nod, she went back to looking through the refrigerator. "Got any ideas for dinner?"

"Well, as Leo always says, 'The eggs of today are better than the chickens of tomorrow.'"

Surprised by how much the quote did sound like something Leo would say, Amy stopped digging through the refrigerator and looked back at Greg. "Did he really say that?"

"Beats me." He nodded toward the refrigerator. "How about those eggs you got today?"

"Sounds good to me." Amy pulled out the carton, a bottle of milk, cheese and a bunch of young onions. "I've always liked omelets, but I'll warn you, mine end up looking more like scrambled eggs."

"No problem. Anything besides a meal out of a can will taste good to me."

As she gathered everything she needed, Amy tried to ignore Greg's nearness. Her attempt was futile. She could feel his gaze and sense his embarrassment over what had happened earlier.

Hers was as great.

He'd kissed her, and she'd kissed him back. Neither could deny it had happened. Nor explain why. They simply had to go on.

She picked up the conversation as she diced the onions. "So what do *you* think of *Lyon's Pride* lately?"

He leaned on his crutches, watching her. "I thought it was getting a message across. Others seem to think the message was too harsh."

"Harsh isn't the word for it." She stopped chopping and turned his way. "It's more like he has an ax to grind."

"Maybe that ax needs to be ground."

"Maybe the guy who draws that strip needs to spend some time with a doctor, see what a doctor's life is really like."

"You offering to take him in?"

She grinned. "Sure, why not? A week here and I don't think he'd be portraying doctors as lazy and money hungry."

Amy wasn't sure how to describe the look Greg gave her. Intense. Penetrating. Probing. It made her nervous. "Don't look at me that way."

"What way's that?" he asked, his eyebrows rising.

As though you're reaching into my soul, she wanted to say. "The way you're looking at me."

"So, how should I look at you?" He frowned. Then smiled a silly grin. Then glared. Then widened his eyes in surprise. He looked like a cartoon character, each expression exaggerated.

Amy simply stared at him, her own mouth slightly open.

"Stop me when I hit a way of looking at you that you like."

She couldn't hold back the laughter. "You're crazy, you know that?"

"Maybe." He was feeling a little nutty. For one insane moment he was actually considering staying on with her, to see what she did when she paid her house calls. But only for a moment.

When the rain stopped, he'd be on his way. "Need some help?"

"Sure. You can set the table. That is, if you think you can do it without breaking all of my dishes."

"Hey, I'm getting pretty good on these things. Another day and I'll be ready to take you dancing."

"We'd make a great team," she said sarcastically.

"Ah-ah," he chastised and extended one crutch, lightly tapping her bad leg with the tip. "Leo says, 'The lion who sees only the thorns, misses the beauty of the rose.'"

"Meaning?" She thought she knew, but selfishly she wanted to hear it from him.

"Meaning you have a beautiful vase of roses upstairs. From your stone carver?"

He was probing. He was also changing the subject, and she knew to go back would make her look vain. Her answer was honest. "A gift from Miss Emily. She has a hothouse and raises roses."

Greg blessed Miss Emily's roses. "And what about your stone carver? Does he send you flowers?"

Amy finished the onions and scraped them into the frying pan. "Aaron's not exactly the flower-sending type."

"And what type is Aaron?"

"The practical type."

"And he doesn't mind your having a man staying with you?" Greg knew *he* certainly would.

"Aaron's away, visiting a sister in Oregon. He won't be back for a month," Amy explained. "Besides, I told you last night, we're just friends. Last winter we worked together on a committee to improve health awareness, and I've gone with him a couple of times when he's delivered a gravestone."

"That doesn't sound like a very romantic date."

She didn't tell him it was about as romantic as she'd had in a long time, and that she'd given up looking for romantic. The problem was, now that she'd been kissed, truly kissed, she knew she'd never be satisfied with less. Gregory Lyman might be gone in a few days, but she would remember the two times he'd kissed her for as long as she lived.

Chapter Six

"You're quite the cook," Greg said, finishing the last of his omelet.

Amy was staring at her plate. She'd been pushing pieces of egg around ever since she'd sat down, and he didn't think she'd eaten more than two bites. He knew she was still upset over his kissing her, then stopping, and he felt guilty. "I don't suppose you'd appreciate the old cliché that someday you'll make some man a wonderful wife."

She looked up, the pain he was causing her all too evident in those lovely green eyes. "You will," he said softly. "I'm just not the right man."

She stiffened and set down her fork. "Who said I was looking for a man?"

Her kisses did. The hungry, unbridled passion she offered did. And the anguish he'd seen when he rejected her unspoken offer did.

"You didn't," he said. "I just wanted you to understand that the problem is with me, not you."

"Actually, there's no problem at all," she insisted, forcing a smile. "To be honest, I don't have time for a man. Did you notice the wooden thermometer out on the lawn in front of the clinic?"

He shook his head. If it had been there the night before, he hadn't seen it. All he'd been aware of going from Mel's truck to the X-ray room was pain...and the woman beside him.

"To keep me here in Wyngate, the townspeople have started a fund drive. By June thirtieth they need enough money or pledges to know they can keep this clinic running another year without the financial backing of the hospital in Bedford. If they don't make it, I'm out of a job and a home. The thermometer's red indicator tells us how close we are to reaching our goal. So, for the next month and a half, besides running a medical practice, I'll be attending the meetings of every organization you can name around Wyngate—trying to get their financial support—serving at spaghetti dinners and putting the final touches on the auction we're holding the end of June. All that leaves me much too busy for romance."

"Making us just two ships passing in the night. Is that it?"

"That's about it. My ship is trying to save a clinic, yours is—?"

"I'm trying to improve my vision."

"Your vision?" Her attention snapped to his eyes. "What's wrong with your vision?"

"My friend Brian says I'm myopic, that I see only what I want to see. He told me I need to make some changes or my career will be finished."

"Your career as a messenger?"

Greg grinned at the way she'd phrased the question. The lady was smart. She hadn't bought his messenger story. Not one bit. He was half tempted to tell her the truth, but since it was still raining outside, and he had no desire to be kicked out of a warm house this late at night, he decided to play it safe. "Messengers sometimes need to expand their horizons. I decided to take a walk."

"A walk across the United States." She stopped pretending she was going to eat the omelet. "Tell me, how did you get into this messenger business anyway?"

He thought quickly. If he framed his answers carefully, he could be honest yet not tell too much. "A friend suggested it. She said I showed talent and should give it a try."

"A talent for delivering messages?"

"Right." He grinned. "I mean, really, not everyone can do it. I had to draw upon past experiences."

"Past experiences?" Amy knew he was alluding to something that had nothing to do with delivering messages, but she had absolutely no idea what that might be. "And is there a lot of business for messengers in New York City?"

"I was plenty busy for almost ten years, but lately some people haven't liked what I've been doing and that hasn't been good."

"So you quit? Got out of town?"

A trickle of fear—not for herself but for him—entered her thoughts. What he'd been saying was beginning to come together. He'd been in communications. He'd been a messenger. And he'd worked in New York City.

Not all messages were verbal or written.

Cautiously, she asked, "This messenger business, is it...was it dangerous?"

"More what I'd call unpredictable."

"Maybe..." She paused, carefully searching for the right words. "Maybe a little on the shady side?"

He had a feeling he knew what she was thinking. He played along. "Some of it's a little shady, but I drew the line on what I would do."

"Just what would you do?"

He couldn't keep it up. She looked too worried. "Nothing illegal, Amy. I wasn't a messenger for the Mafia or anything like that."

"No drugs were involved?" She laughed but looked relieved.

"Absolutely no drugs."

"I knew it. You don't have any tracks on your arms."

"You checked?"

"I may be naive, but I'm not stupid." She made no pretense of hiding her curiosity. "You're not going to tell me what you do, are you?"

He faked a look of innocence. "I did tell you. I am—was a messenger."

"A nearsighted one." She shook her head. "So, has your walk cross-country been helping your vision?"

"Not the way Brian had hoped, but I am finding it interesting. For one thing, other than the two years I was in the army and was stationed in Georgia, I never had been out of New York City. Some of the people I've talked to in the last forty-seven days have been fascinating."

"Once it stops raining, you'll have to take a look around Wyngate. I think you'll find it quite different from New York City, and its residents equally fascinating." She grinned, but he knew the affection she had for the town and its people.

"I just might do that."

Pushing back her chair, she stood. "Well, if you'll excuse me, as soon as I do these dishes, I'm going to go to bed. It's been a long day."

And she'd had a short night the night before. Greg knew she had to be exhausted. "Forget the dishes. I'll do them."

He carried his own plate to the sink. He was getting quite good at maneuvering on crutches, even if he did say so himself.

She tensed when he stopped by her side. It was just a slight tightening of her shoulders and an almost imperceptible holding of her breath, but he noticed.

Maybe they weren't right for each other, but there was definitely some kind of chemistry working between them. He was sure it was something he could control and ignore; yet simply being close to her, he wanted to reach out and touch her, brush the backs of his fingers over the scars on her cheeks, and turn her face toward him, so he could look into those beautiful expressive eyes of hers.

He held his own breath, gripping his plate.

"I...I think I will let you do the dishes," she said in a rush. Not once looking at him, she limped toward the doorway to the hall.

He watched her go. She was running from her feelings and he couldn't stop her, not without hurting her more. At the doorway she paused and did look back. Her expression was friendly and composed. It was her eyes that held the longing. "Have a good night's sleep," she offered.

"Same to you," he returned.

He knew neither of them would.

It was after nine the next morning when Greg woke. During his mostly sleepless night he'd made up his mind. Rain or no rain, he was leaving. He didn't understand the attraction he felt for Amy, but considering everything, his staying would only hurt her.

He'd leave while she was busy seeing patients, leave her a note and some money and take off. Surely someone would give him a ride to the next decent-sized town.

Twenty minutes later, Greg was dressed and ready to go. His sleeping bag once again a part of his backpack, he hoisted it up on his back, tested his stability on the crutches, then went to the kitchen to find a sheet of paper and a pencil or pen to leave a note.

On the counter he found one from her, along with several boxes of cereal and instructions on how to use the coffeepot.

On the road he usually had a high-energy bar for breakfast and grabbed some coffee at the first gas station he came to. The idea of fresh-perked coffee and milk and cereal—in a bowl—sounded good. Very good. Slipping his pack off his shoulders, he left it in a corner and started the coffee.

He had it brewing and had just pulled the milk jug from the refrigerator when the back door opened and a harsh, strident voice pierced the solitude of the kitchen. "What are y'doin' here?" Startled, Greg lost his grip on the milk jug. He made a grab for it, only to hit his armpit on the top of the crutch and come up short. With a thud the jug landed on the linoleum. Off popped the top.

Within seconds he was standing in a puddle of milk.

"Now look what y've done!" scolded Peggy.

He felt like a six-year-old being reprimanded by his mother. Damn the woman for coming up on him like that! Yelling at him! Surprising him!

Without a word, he pushed the refrigerator door closed and swung his crutches around to go to the sink for a rag.

"Stand where y'are!" Peggy ordered.

Obediently he stopped, but his words were terse. "I'm going to get a rag."

"All y're goin' t'do is track milk all over th' floor." With an exasperated sigh, she set her purse down on the far end of the counter and marched past him. "I'll take care of it."

For years his mother had used that same martyred tone. How she'd loved to make him feel guilty. For being sick. For not loving her enough. For wanting to leave. She'd been a master manipulator, but he had a feeling Peggy was as good. Only he wasn't about to be manipulated. "I can handle this myself."

She scoffed. "Sure, like y'handled getting that milk. Next thing y'know, you'll slip and break y'other leg." She grabbed two dish towels from a drawer and tossed them over the puddle of milk. Moving closer, she watched him leerily. He remembered what Amy had said and tried to reassure the woman. "I'm not on drugs."

Peggy snorted and kneeled beside him.

"You surprised me," he explained. "I didn't think you worked today. I didn't know you were around."

She swiped one towel over his shoe. "I came back t'see if I needed t'pick up more milk f'r tomorrow. Obviously, I do." Standing, the dripping, milk-soaked towels in her hands, she looked at his backpack, then at him. "Y're leavin'?"

"As soon as I have breakfast."

"Does she know?"

"I was going to leave her a note."

Peggy snorted again. "Just like a man. Waits 'til a woman's back is turned, then runs off."

"I thought you didn't approve of my being here?"

"I don't," Peggy said. "On th' other hand, I saw th' way she looked when she talked about you yesterday. The way she was all kinda protective about you. Seems like after all she's done f'r you, y'could at least stay long enough t'say goodbye t'her face."

Guilt. It was a powerful tool in the hands of an expert, and Peggy was definitely an expert. "All right, I'll stay until lunchtime and tell her. Face-to-face."

With a half laugh, Peggy carried the towels to the sink. Her back to him, she began rinsing them out and squeezing them dry. Greg stood where he was, afraid if he moved, he'd be yelled at. "What else should I do?" he asked.

"Why ask me?" she asked, barely glancing over her shoulder, her disapproval evident in every twist she gave the towels.

Why indeed? he wondered. "My staying would only hurt her."

"I'm not telling you t'stay." She came back to where he stood. "I'm tellin' you not t'hurt her. Don't leave her feelin' used."

"Nothing's happened between us," he insisted, though he knew that wasn't entirely true. Perhaps they hadn't made love, but something had happened between them. It happened every time they were together.

Peggy eyed him suspiciously, then kneeled and wiped over the floor again. In moments she had the last of the milk up. Standing, she faced him. "That will do 'til tomorrow. Then I'll give this floor a good moppin' and waxin'."

The towels were given one more rinsing, then went into a laundry basket. He thought she would leave, but instead Peggy came back into the kitchen. For a moment she stood and looked him over—from his hair to the toes sticking out of his cast—then she scowled. "Didn't Doc Amy tell you t'keep that foot up?"

"For a day or two. Yes."

"So, go sit down," Peggy ordered, waving a hand toward the kitchen table. "Get it up. I'll get you y're coffee."

"I can get it myself," he insisted.

"Sure, and spill it. Sit!"

Shaking his head, his curls spilling across his shoulders, Greg went over to the table and sat. Still feeling like a six-year-old, he lifted his right leg up onto a chair.

And was glad to be off his feet.

Peggy brought him his coffee, the boxes of cereal that Amy had left out on the counter, a bowl and what was left of the milk. And while he fixed his breakfast, she checked the refrigerator and wrote several items down on a list she took from her purse. When she was finished, she turned to him. "I don't know if y'realize it, but things aren't good f'r Doc Amy. If we're gonna keep her here in Wyngate, we're all gonna have t'pitch in. She can't afford to feed and care for a freeloader."

"I'll pay her." He glanced down at his near-empty cereal bowl. "For everything."

"Y'do that."

After Peggy left, Greg mopped the entire kitchen floor, and by the time he figured Amy would be finished in the clinic, he'd opened and heated a large can of vegetable soup that he'd had in his pack. If she could put food out for him, he could do the same for her.

Amy smelled the soup the moment she stepped through the door from the clinic and into the hallway. "Wow, something smells good," she called out.

"Lunch is served, madam." Greg came to the kitchen doorway, bowed his head and doffed an imaginary hat.

"Such service." She tried to ignore the tingly sensation of pure joy that washed through her, along with the queasiness in her stomach. If she didn't know better, she'd swear she was coming down with something. That, or a thousand butterflies had taken up residence in her abdominal cavity. All because a man with long, blond hair and a nice set of legs was wearing an apron . . . and cooking lunch for her.

She'd hated the feeling of pleasure she'd experienced when she woke that morning and saw it was still raining. Hated wanting to rush through the patients in the clinic so she could get back and see Greg, talk to him. Now she knew what she would hate most of all was the day she came back and he was no longer around.

"How are you feeling?" she asked in as professional a tone as she could muster.

"Not bad at all. Certainly better than yesterday." He flexed his shoulders, and his arm muscles rippled. The butterflies inside of her made a magnificent swoop.

He suggested she serve her own soup rather than chance his spilling it, then as she did, he told her about Peggy stopping by and surprising him and how he'd spilled half a bottle of her milk that morning. She could tell he was uneasy about something. While she ate, he talked more than he ever had since they'd met—about people he'd met while on the road, places he'd slept and things he'd seen. He laughed a lot, but it was a tight, forced laugh.

It wasn't until she took her bowl to the sink that she noticed his backpack sitting by the back door. Then she knew why he was tense.

He was leaving.

She looked out the window, a knot in her throat making it impossible for her to swallow. She'd thought she would have some time with him, another night at least. She'd been wrong.

Slowly she turned and faced him. "It's still raining."

He nodded, understanding what she was saying. "I've got to go."

"Why?"

"You know."

All she knew was she'd loved it when he'd looked at her as though she were beautiful. Had loved it when he'd held her in his arms. Kissed her.

She also knew she was kidding herself if she thought he actually saw her as anything more than a woman with scars and a limp. To ask him to stay would only lead to pain...and more scars.

"You're probably right," she said.

Her answer surprised Greg, and he frowned. He'd expected her to ask him to stay, to plead with him to stay. To cry. That was what his mother had always done when he'd said he wanted to leave. "No arguments?"

"What can I say?" She nodded toward the back door and his pack. "You've obviously already made up your mind. There are some garbage bags under the sink. Wrap one around that cast so it doesn't get wet."

She limped out of the kitchen and he stared after her. He didn't move from his chair, even after he heard her go up the stairs. It was crazy. He was the one leaving, yet he felt he'd been left.

The gray sky and rain didn't improve his mood. He watched the raindrops trickle down the windowpanes, and wondered how he was going to continue his crusade on crutches. With a garbage bag on his leg, no less. The woman didn't care if he looked like an idiot. Or if he fell and broke his other leg. Here he'd thought he'd found one doctor who was different. She wasn't. Probably if he talked to her patients, he'd find out they all liked her so much because she passed out pills like candy. Don't worry about a patient's health and well-being. Just keep them happy.

He was angry by the time she came back down the stairs. "Can I give you a ride anywhere?" she asked. "My first call is north of town."

"I'm going with you."

"Fine." She glanced at his cast. "You really need to wrap that to keep it from getting wet."

"I mean I'm going with you when you make your calls."

She frowned. "I don't understand."

If she was confused by his statement, he didn't blame her. He was a little confused himself. Yet it seemed to make perfectly good sense. "A doctor who makes house calls is unique nowadays. I want to go along and see just how you do this."

He thought she'd say no, tell him it was impossible, bring up a patient's right to privacy and all of that. She did seem to think about it, then, to his surprise, she grinned. "That's absolutely perfect. I'll get my things in the car while you wrap that cast."

Chapter Seven

"Why make house calls? Why not simply let people come to you?" Greg asked, though he had to admit, the rolling hills, woods and farmland they were driving through were beautiful and if he had the choice, he'd choose cruising a rural road to being stuck in a clinic.

"I believe in a holistic approach to medicine," Amy explained. "The way a person lives—his home environment, job, friends—it all plays a part in his well-being. Or lack of it. Also, some of the people around here won't come to a doctor's office, not unless they're practically dying. Some believe the home remedies they know are just as good as anything I might have in my office. Which may or may not be true. I've just found that a lot of grief and pain can be avoided if I 'happen' to stop by."

He didn't buy her story. She was drumming up business. That's what she was doing. If patients wouldn't come to her, she'd go to them. And here everyone thought she was so noble, the small-town doctor willing to treat anyone. The *poor* doctor who needed the town's help and money. Lots of money.

He had to have injured his head as well as his ankle for him not to have seen how much Amy was just like all the other doctors he'd dealt with. He had looked at the scars on her face and thought she was different. Had let an occasional blush delude him into thinking of her as sweet and innocent.

What she was was a serpent, quietly wrapping herself around the hearts and souls of everyone in this town. The squeeze would come when they least expected it. He felt a tightening around his own heart.

Amy couldn't understand but she could feel Greg's anger. Something had triggered it, something that happened between the time he'd said he was leaving and when he'd said he was going with her, but she didn't have the slightest idea what it was. In her defense, she tried to explain her plan for the afternoon.

"In case you're wondering, we're going to be seeing Velma Tabor. Actually, it's her husband, Vern, she's worried about. Velma's sixty-seven and Vern's in his seventies. He won't come to me because I'm a woman."

Greg nodded. It was as he'd suspected. If a potential patient wouldn't come to her, she'd go to him.

"Not that that bothers me," she continued. "Vern has his own doctors in Bedford. Several, I guess. But Velma says lately his memory has been getting worse and worse and he's doing strange things, talking constantly and saying things he normally never would say. She's afraid he has Alzheimer's."

Greg leaned back in his seat and crossed his arms over his chest. "So you're going to drop by, give him a few pills and make everything just fine for Velma, is that it? Keep old Vern from bothering her. Make a new recruit."

"No." Amy didn't like the way Greg's question sounded like an accusation. "I have no desire to recruit any more patients. I'm busy enough as it is. But Vern's behavior is affecting Velma's health. And she *is* my patient."

He glanced her way. It wasn't the response he'd expected. "Then what are you going to do this afternoon?"

"You and I are going to stop by the Tabor house for some of Velma's marvelous rhubarb pie."

Greg grimaced. He'd had rhubarb pie once, and it had been anything but marvelous. He began to regret his impulsive idea of coming along. Confirming beliefs was one thing; subjecting his insides to torture was another.

"This is strictly a social call, you understand," she continued. "But while we're there, I am going to ask Vern a few questions, do a little observing. I hope I can come up with an idea. Otherwise, I don't know what I'm going to do. All I know is Velma was really upset when I saw her at church last Sunday, and if she doesn't get some rest, she's going to end up in a hospital bed."

"Isn't it against the husband's rights for you to barge into his house and start giving him medical advice?"

"I'm not about to give him medical advice, not unless he specifically asks me for some. And I'm not barging in. Velma invited me here today." Amy pulled into a driveway that led to a small white, boxlike wood house set back by a stand of dogwoods. Turning off the ignition, she looked at Greg. "I agreed to your coming along because I think having you with me will make this look like it really is a social call, like we're here for rhubarb pie, and that's all. So please, don't let on that this is anything but."

He grinned a broad grin. "I'll be ever so sociable."

Amy got out of the car and waited for Greg to get up on his crutches. Although it had warmed some from two days before, the wind was still chilly and the rain was coming down at a steady rate. She had to stretch and Greg had to duck for her to hold an umbrella over both of them. Together they headed for the house.

"Also," she warned as they neared the door. "I don't want *you* giving any medical advice."

"Don't worry. If I gave any advice, it would be to stay away from you doctors."

"You didn't seem to mind seeing a doctor the other night when Mel brought you to my door."

"That was different." Greg was clearly defensive. "I just don't trust doctors when they start writing prescriptions."

Amy realized that would explain his reticence to take anything for pain. He hadn't been playing the macho male; he'd been afraid of what she might give him.

Vern Tabor greeted them at the door. The first thing Amy noticed was the old man's white hair was practically standing on end, making him look like a short-haired Albert Einstein. The second thing she noticed was his pupils were dilated.

He started talking the moment he saw them. "Velma said you was comin' by. She's been fussin' all mornin'." He laughed, but eyed Amy suspiciously. "That woman's always worryin' about this and that. Tellin' me I need to go see you. She didn't ask you to come see me, did she?"

"This is strictly a social call," Amy lied. "You know I can't resist Velma's rhubarb pie."

"She's the one who needs to see you," Vern went on, stepping back into the house and motioning for them to come in. "All she does is nag, nag, nag. You got anything to stop a woman from naggin'?"

Vern gave Greg a good looking-over, making a wry face when his gaze was on Greg's hair and frowning at the garbage bag covering Greg's cast.

Amy made the introductions.

"Hain't seen you around Wyngate before," Vern said, again eyeing Greg's hair.

"He's not from around here, Mr. Tabor," she explained. "He was hiking cross-country when he fell down the hill over near Miss Emily's and broke his ankle. He's staying with me for a few days."

"Until the rain stops," Greg added.

"From what the weatherman says, you'll be stayin' awhile. Give you a chance to get that hair cut." Vern turned away and headed for the kitchen.

Greg chuckled, and Amy smiled and looked around. The Tabors' house was small and the furnishings were old, but there were flowers on the fireplace mantel and not a speck of dust anywhere. "You have a lovely home," she called after Vern.

"Rat hole, that's what it is," he grumbled and sat down at the kitchen table. "Come on in and set down. Velma will be out shortly. She's fussin', as usual."

Velma Tabor came out of a bedroom at that moment, patting a circle of tight gray curls and smiling nervously. She was a small woman and her fluttery motions always made Amy think of a hummingbird. Velma sighed when she saw Amy. "You're here."

"Wouldn't miss a piece of your rhubarb pie," Amy said loud enough for Vern to hear. "It was nice of you to invite me to stop by before I start my calls."

It took a few minutes before everyone was seated around the kitchen table. Velma got an extra chair and a pillow so Greg could elevate his ankle, then brought the pie to the table. Vern scoffed at his wife's warning that he'd had enough caffeine and poured himself another cup of coffee. Velma offered a tea she'd made from dried raspberry leaves and mint. Amy had a cup, but Greg declined. He went with Vern's coffee, but Amy noticed he didn't take more than two sips. He did much better on the rhubarb pie. His first bite was tentative, his second bolder, and from then on the pie disappeared at a steady rate. The moment he finished,

Velma offered him another slice. There was no hesitation on Greg's part, and Amy had to suppress a grin as his second piece disappeared almost as quickly as the first.

All the while, Vern talked constantly, often repeating himself. Amy listened and observed—that was what she was there for—and soon she had a pretty good idea of what was wrong. It was only a matter of guiding the conversation in the direction she wanted, and hoping Vern wasn't so over-stimulated he'd miss what he needed to see.

She also watched Greg, aware that he was also keeping a close eye on her. He said nothing, but she could feel him waiting for her to do or say the wrong thing. He'd become her judge and jury, and she didn't like it.

It took over an hour before Amy got Vern to show her all of the medicine he was taking. Then slowly, carefully, she explained what each pill did and what happened when they were mixed. Before they were ready to leave, she made out a list of all his medication and had him promise he'd show the list to each of his doctors within the next week.

At the door, Velma hugged her, tears coming to the older woman's eyes. "You really think it's the pills, Doc Amy? Not Alzheimer's?"

"I think that's all it is."

"Stop your blubbering," Vern chastised, but nodded at Amy. "I want you to know, it's not 'cause of how you look that I don't go see you," he said. "But if Velma here's happy seeing a woman doctor, that's fine with me."

"Thank you, Vern." Amy shook his hand and so did Greg. Back in the car, she turned to him. "Okay. So, what's your diagnosis?"

"That his doctor should have asked the questions you asked."

"You're right. Vern also should have told his doctors what each was prescribing rather than assuming they would know. Why are you so anti-doctor?"

"Because doctors killed my mother."

His answer surprised and bothered her. She started the car and headed back to town before she asked her next question. "How?"

He made a sound that was half grunt, half sigh, and looked out the side window. "Too many doctors didn't take the time to care. They labeled my mother a hypochondriac and a bother. They took her money and they gave her prescriptions for medication. Some pills made her happy. Some let her sleep. She died in her sleep. Drunk and happy."

"Greg, I'm not trying to defend what those doctors did, but it sounds like your mother needed a psychiatrist."

Out of the corner of her eye, she could see him look at her, then back out the side window. "She had one. And you're right, of course, she *was* crazy."

"I didn't mean—" she started, but he interrupted.

"No, you are right. She was bonkers. There are times I even wonder why I'm so upset with what happened to her. Maybe, considering everything she did, she deserved to die. Except, I just don't feel that way."

"No one deserves to die," Amy insisted.

Turning in his seat, Greg faced her again. "The thing is, her doctors should have known what she would do with those pills."

"We're not gods, Greg. We're not all-seeing, all-knowing. Few doctors have the luxury I have to spend two hours in a patient's home, eating rhubarb pie and drinking tea. Most of the time we can only go on what we see, what we hear and what we know. Maybe your mother's doctors shouldn't have prescribed the pills they did. I don't know. I do know they probably thought they were doing the best they could for her."

He stared at her in silence, then looked straight ahead. She knew he didn't believe her. She wished she didn't care.

"My next stop is south of town," she said as they neared the clinic. "I'll drop you off first."

"No, I want to go with you."

"You can't," she said firmly. "This one is an actual patient."

"Afraid to let me see what you do with an *actual* patient?"

"No, but—" She thought about where she was going. Molly wouldn't care if she brought Greg along. Molly would think it was a kick, and so would the children. Slyly, Amy smiled. "Okay. Just don't blame me."

"Blame you?"

"I'm going to see Molly Brighton." As long as she wasn't going to drop Greg off at the house, Amy swung off the main highway and headed for the back roads that would take her to the Brighton house. "Molly's seven months pregnant and has three children. All at home. All under the age of five."

Greg chuckled. "Her husband believe in keeping her barefoot and pregnant?"

"Molly seems to want a lot of children as much as David does. They moved here from Indianapolis. They see themselves as new-age settlers, going back to a time when families were large and the land supplied everything one needed. I think you'll find this an interesting experience."

His experience began the moment he stepped through the doorway and was attacked by four-year-old Todd and three-year-old Daniel. Fourteen-month-old Christine ran crying to the couch and buried her head against her mother's oversized belly. As soon as introductions were made and raincoats removed, Amy helped Molly and the shy toddler from the couch to the bedroom. To her relief, Greg didn't follow, though Amy had a feeling Molly wouldn't have objected.

"Now that's a good-looking man," Molly said the moment Amy closed the bedroom door.

"A woman in your condition is not supposed to notice other men," Amy chastised and went to the bathroom to scrub her hands.

Molly called after her, laughing. "Hey, I'm pregnant, not dead. Where did you pick him up?"

"Mel brought him to the clinic the other night. Greg fell down the hill by Miss Emily's pumpkin patch and broke his ankle."

"Love that hair of his."

Amy came back into the room, drying her hands. "You know what's crazy, sometimes I look at him, with all that hair and that beard, and I think of a lion."

"About to pounce on you?" Molly asked, sparks of pure curiosity in her brown eyes.

"Hardly," she insisted and pulled some tongue depressors out of her bag for Christine to play with. With the child occupied, Amy began her examination.

Greg wouldn't be pouncing on her today, she realized. Or probably any other day. The romantic who had kissed her so passionately the night before was gone. In his place was a cynic.

"I hear you and Aaron had a fight," Molly said.

"You heard wrong," Amy insisted. "His sister just had a baby. He went back to see her."

"Grace Danville stopped by the other day. She brought the children some old books from the library. She said she thought you and Aaron should get married."

"Seems quite a few people have come up with that idea lately," Amy admitted. Aaron included. "It wouldn't work."

"I don't think so, either," Molly agreed, then chuckled. "How 'bout your lion?"

Amy glanced toward the closed door. "Greg?" Slowly she shook her head. "He's the kind of guy who would go for my sister, not me. Besides, he's just passing through. As soon as this rain stops, he'll be on his way."

"Too bad." Molly nudged Amy with her foot. "Don't go selling yourself short. You've got a lot to offer a guy. How is your sister doing, anyway?"

Molly had met Chris a few months before. The two women had hit it off instantly, but Amy didn't know anyone who didn't like Molly. "Chris's law career is doing great. Her divorce, however, is really getting her down. I guess Brad is contesting everything. She's planning on coming down again sometime this summer."

"You'll have to bring her by."

The sound of the boys yelling in the other room turned Amy's attention back to the door. "Poor guy," Molly said, then laughed. "Did you warn him about what he was getting into?"

"He was the one who insisted on coming." Though she doubted he'd truly understood what he was getting into. But it was nice to have someone in the other room and not have to stop every few minutes in her examination to check on the boys for Molly. At least she hoped Greg wouldn't let them kill each other.

When the yelling turned to laughter, curiosity got the best of Christine. Leaving her pile of tongue depressors, she fussed until Amy opened the door. For a moment the child simply watched from the safety of the bedroom, and so did Amy. Greg was seated on the couch, where Molly had been earlier, his leg propped up. Without moving more than a few inches at a time, he twisted and turned, making threatening gestures with his hands. Over and over again Greg growled and the boys giggled and backed off, then came close again, loving the game.

"He definitely looks like a lion now," Amy said, and turned back to Molly. "A cornered lion. And your boys have him at bay."

Christine toddled out into the living room, and Amy pushed the door closed and continued her examination. It wasn't until they realized how quiet it had become in the other room that the two women looked toward the door. "What did he do, tie them up and gag them?" Molly asked.

"I don't know. I'll go see." Amy again left Molly's side and cracked open the door to peek out.

Greg was still on the couch, his cast propped up on a pillow. On his lap he had an oversized book that he was using as a drawing board and several sheets of typing paper. In his hand, he held a crayon, and around him were all three children. He was talking to each, his voice softly threatening. While he talked, he drew. Wide-eyed, they watched him.

Amy smiled and walked back to Molly. "The man amazes me. Now, he's drawing pictures."

Chapter Eight

Greg was certain the buzzards circling high above thought the small red car weaving back and forth down the narrow road was a creature in distress. Amy licked her lips as she skillfully avoided each pothole, and the distress was his. How could he distrust this woman? How could he keep from wanting her? She put her all into everything she did.

"You can see why it's easier for me to go to them than it is for them to come to me," Amy said, swinging the wheel to the left and throwing him her way.

He groaned and bounced toward her, and she glanced his way. "Sorry. Someday they'll resurface this road."

"Any reason why we're competing in the Indy 500?"

She darted a look at the speedometer, then eased her foot off the gas. "Habit, I guess."

Tension, she knew, would be a better answer. Greg made her tense. Confused her. Nothing made sense about the man. Not the way he made her feel inside, his changing his mind about leaving that afternoon, his anger or even his explanation of what he did for a living. "You're quite an artist . . . for a messenger."

Her pause had been deliberate, and she once again glanced his way, waiting for an explanation.

"Haven't you heard?" he said. "A picture's worth a thousand words. My drawings make it easier for me to get my messages across."

"That so? What message were you trying to get across with those monsters you drew for Todd and Daniel?"

"That if they didn't stop jumping all over me, I was going to call in the monsters to eat them up."

"You told them that?" She looked shocked.

Greg relaxed back in his seat and smiled. "You'll have to ask them."

They rode in silence for a while. He kept trying to think of anything Amy had done that afternoon that he could fault. Not one thing came to mind. At Molly's, after Amy came out of the bedroom, she took a few minutes to check each of the children, looking into their eyes, listening to their hearts and lungs. Talking to them. How different his life would have been if just one doctor had taken the time to stop by his house, had listened to those lungs his mother insisted were clogged and frail. Had talked to him.

Turning his head to the side, he watched Amy drive. He'd started this cross-country walk to smell the flowers, as Brian had suggested, but soon his goal had changed. It hadn't taken him long to realize his walk was a great way to gather information. It was amazing how willing people were to talk about problems they'd had with their doctors. In the forty-seven days he was on the road, he'd heard hundreds of stories of misdiagnoses, operations that never should have taken place and doctors who only cared if their bills—exorbitant bills—would be paid, not if the patient lived or died. He'd truly begun to believe he was right, that there weren't any good doctors around.

Now he'd found one.

"What made you decide to go into medicine?" he asked.

"This." She patted her short leg. "And the operations I had to go through to put my face back together."

There was a touch of sorrow in her eyes when she looked his way. "If you think my face looks bad now, you should have seen what I looked like after the accident."

"I don't think your face looks bad."

He wanted her to believe him and brushed the backs of his fingers over her cheeks. The moment he did, he knew he shouldn't have. Maybe he didn't want to like her, but the chemistry was still there, the electricity. He felt it pulse through his body and heard the quick intake of her breath. She tried to cover it up with a laugh.

"I can tell you one thing for sure, I won't be winning any beauty pageants." Not like her sister had. "And it took a lot of operations to get me to this point. From the age of eight to ten, I lived in the hospital. I guess it was inevitable I'd either never want to see another hospital again or I'd grow up wanting to be a doctor."

Two years in a hospital. Two years of her childhood lost. He understood what that meant. "So now you're Wyngate's Angel of Mercy, driving from house to house, dispensing medicine and a little common sense."

"Wyngate's a great place to work."

From what he'd seen, he wasn't sure about that. There didn't seem to be any industry, no new houses were being built, and a lot of families lived in trailers. "This is not exactly a thriving metropolis. No dreams of working in a big city? Of having a regular practice? Fancy office? Patients who pay with money instead of eggs?"

She shook her head to each possibility. "None whatsoever. This place is as close to perfect as I could find." Amy paused. "Well, maybe not quite perfect. It would have been nice if the hospital hadn't had cutbacks and I didn't have to go to the community, begging for money. And that X-ray machine I have is the pits. I'd love to get a new one."

"And how much will that cost?"

"Between one and two hundred thousand. I'd just started pricing them when the hospital informed me that they were going to close the clinic. When we have the auction at the end of June, I'm hoping we'll have raised enough money to run the clinic and to start a fund for an X-ray machine."

"You really think you'll make all that much from an auction?"

"I'm hoping." She crossed her fingers. "Barbara, my friend who's handling the publicity, has all sorts of good ideas."

"And if you don't make your goal? Don't even make enough to keep the clinic going?"

She glanced his way, then straight ahead. "I don't know. I guess I start job hunting."

When Amy pulled up to her garage, Greg saw the wooden thermometer on the lawn in front of the clinic. The red indicator of how much had been collected was halfway to the top. Her talk might be optimistic, but she still had a long way to go and only seven weeks in which to succeed.

Turning off the ignition, she faced him. "So, did you see what you wanted to see this afternoon?"

"Maybe."

He was more relaxed than when they'd left the house. Or perhaps, Amy decided, he was just too tired to be ornery. Molly's children had kept him busy, climbing all over him, pestering him for more drawings of dragons and monsters. Greg might have threatened the boys a little, but Amy didn't think Todd or Daniel took those threats seriously. And once Christine got over her shyness, she'd stuck to Greg like a burr. The man did have a way with children.

"So are you going to stay another night?" she asked, not quite sure what she wanted him to answer. Stay, and she was in danger of falling deeper under his spell. Go, and she would be left with only memories.

He looked out the window at the gray sky. "It's stopped raining."

"But it could start again."

It was then that her beeper went off. She hesitated a moment, waiting for Greg's answer. Again the beeper sounded, and she opened the car door. "I have to check on this. It might be an emergency."

By the time Greg entered the kitchen, Amy was on the phone. Even as she talked, she was taking off her raincoat. The moment she replaced the receiver, she turned to Greg. "Eldon Cole's wife is bringing their son Nate over. He stepped on a nail."

She knew what she wanted to ask. She just didn't want to sound desperate. "Will you stay? At least until I'm finished with Nate?"

He nodded. "I'll fix something for dinner."

"There are steaks in the freezer," she called as she hurried down the hallway. "Alvin Leehouts brought some over last week."

He watched the door to the clinic close behind her and suddenly the house seemed too quiet. He supposed he could have offered to help her with the boy, but he'd really never been that good about blood and gore. He was willing to let her play doctor, and he'd cook dinner. Then he would leave.

It took an hour from the time he saw the car pull up in front of the clinic to when the boy and his mother left. The way Greg had it timed, he'd give Amy a chance to unwind, maybe shower and change if she liked, then he'd grill the steaks, microwave a couple of potatoes and steam some frozen peas. She'd worked hard. She deserved a good meal.

Greg stared out the kitchen window. It was raining again, a fine, misty rain that made everything look as though it were shrouded in gray gauze. It was also quite cold. The idea of leaving wasn't as appealing as it had been that morning. And maybe he didn't need to go just yet. He'd spent close to five hours with Amy, and during that time he could honestly say he'd treated her like a sister. Perhaps once or twice he'd touched her and felt the urge to kiss her. But he'd resisted.

Whatever the attraction, he could control it. He was sure of that.

"I'm going to take a quick shower," Amy said from behind him.

Greg jerked back from the window. He hadn't heard her come down the hallway.

Off balance, he wobbled, then straightened on the crutches. Selfconsciously, he laughed. "You caught me daydreaming."

"I see it's raining again."

"Yes." He let his gaze drift down from her face to her white lab coat. She was really quite pretty, in spite of the scars and her bad leg.

If he were to draw her, he'd picture her as an impala, her large, expressive eyes dominating her face and her slender body poised for flight. Far too trusting, she gazed at him, and he realized how easily he could kill the spirit in those eyes. She wasn't the enemy; he was.

"I . . . I won't be long."

"Take your time," he said softly.

She limped up the stairs to her bedroom, and he listened to the uneven sound of her steps, heard her opening drawers then closing them. Finally water gurgled in the pipes, and he knew she'd turned on the shower. The idea of her standing naked under a stream of warm water heated his blood. He wasn't interested, he told himself. All he could do was bring her pain. The lion and the impala. It was too ludicrous. Too bizarre.

Nevertheless, he couldn't stop himself from imagining what it would be like to make love with Amy, to kiss away her self-doubts and tell her how beautiful she was. Truly beautiful. Tell her how he loved listening to her when she talked. How her laughter made him want to laugh. And how her smiles stoked internal fires better left smoldering.

"She's got the old lion hot and bothered," he murmured and shook his mane. What he needed to do was think of something else. Something that had nothing to do with the woman upstairs, nothing to do with sex.

He was only halfway successful, and that ended the moment Amy came down the stairs and stepped into the kitchen. "Dinner ready?" she asked, and he sucked in his breath.

She'd put on a dress.

Nervously she stood waiting for his reaction, first clenching her hands into fists, then releasing them and clasping them behind her back. She started to smile, then bit her lower lip, never glancing away from his face.

Slowly he let his gaze move down the front of her. The dress was demure, proper and simple in its lines; yet there was something about its soft peach color that made him think of naked flesh, and something about the way the material molded itself to every curve of her body that triggered a reaction deep in his loins. This was no impala. This was a woman.

He knew she was holding her breath, waiting for him to say something. He could only stammer. "You . . . you look beautiful."

Amy didn't sound much more composed than he felt. "I . . . I thought I should dress." She glanced at the table. "You went to so much trouble."

"No trouble," he insisted. Finding the tablecloth and candle holders had been easy. The trouble he was having was physical. He hoped she'd keep looking at the place settings. Or his face. If her gaze dropped lower, she was going to know exactly what he wanted. And it wasn't food.

He hurried to turn away and start the steaks. She came over and helped with the potatoes. Every time she moved, the scent of her perfume teased him to distraction. This definitely wasn't going to be a relaxed meal. At least not for him.

"Estimated time to dinner—" He checked the clock. "Ten min—"

The ring of the telephone interrupted him. For a moment both Amy and Greg froze. On the second ring, Amy moved and on the third ring, she picked up the receiver. Greg listened, knowing immediately whatever it was, it was serious. When she hung up, she glanced at the table, then back at him.

In her gaze, he saw regret and longing, but he also saw worry and wasn't surprised when she said, "I've got to go. There's been an accident. A tree fell on Tom Gibson."

"What can I do to help?" he offered.

"Nothing." She started toward the hallway. "They've got help coming and an ambulance. I'm just going to grab my bag and a coat and get over there. Go ahead and eat. I don't know when I'll be back."

The steaks were still sizzling when he saw her drive off. The ding of the microwave signaled the potatoes were done, and the aroma of cooked peas filled the kitchen. Alone, Greg grabbed a plate.

Except for a lone light in the living room, the house was dark when Amy returned. She entered through the back door and took off her lab coat. It was covered with mud and so was her dress. In the kitchen, she noted the table was cleared, the dishes washed and a note on the refrigerator said her dinner simply needed to be warmed.

She wasn't in the mood for food.

Soft music came from the living room. Exhausted, she limped into the room to turn off the stereo. What she needed was silence, a stiff drink and a good cry.

She was halfway to the stereo when she saw Greg. He was stretched out on the couch, his cast propped up, the once-pristine white plaster now autographed with the scribbles of Todd, Daniel and Christine.

Greg had slung an arm across his eyes, shielding his face from the light he'd left on. Mesmerized, she stared at him, wanting what she knew she would never have, longing to be able to run her fingers through his thick, tawny hair, and once again feel the strength of his embrace, the pressure of his lips against hers.

As she watched the slow rise and fall of his chest, Amy knew her daydreams might never come true, but at least he was alive. Quietly she turned off the stereo, then grabbed an afghan from the back of a chair. She'd let him sleep on the couch. It was easier than waking him. Easier than talking.

To anyone.

Maybe she could have left without waking him if she hadn't stooped to pull the afghan up under his chin. She'd never know. Before her hand left the blanket, Greg's fingers wrapped around her wrist. "Amy?"

"I was just covering you up."

His voice was gravelly with sleep. "What time is it?"

"Late. I didn't want to wake you."

"No... don't worry." Without releasing his hold on her wrist, he scooted to a sitting position. "How are you? How'd it go? Did you see my note about your dinner?"

"I saw it. I'm... I'm not hungry."

"Amy?" He waited, and she knew he sensed her distress. "What's the matter?"

"He... Tom didn't make it." She felt the tears sting her eyes and hated herself for being so damned emotional. "I'm sorry. You'd think a doctor would get used to seeing death, but I never have.''

''Oh, Amy.'' Greg pulled her down, onto the couch, so she was half sitting half lying across him. Wrapping his arms around her, he cradled her in his embrace. ''Cry if you want. It's all right.''

''I—'' She couldn't talk. The words were a lump in her throat, the memory still so fresh of Tom lying beneath the tree, the life ebbing out of him. It was Tom's wife's crying that had twisted her insides into a knot. The anguished sobs of a woman who had lost her best friend.

''It's all right,'' Greg murmured over and over, his lips brushing against her forehead while his fingers kneaded her back. ''It's all right.''

He held her tight and kept talking, kept kissing her. The words didn't matter, it was the touch of his lips, first against her forehead, then on her cheeks that counted. The feel of his beard brushing against her skin. The scent of him.

He was tenderness. Compassion. Understanding.

He was life.

By the time his mouth covered hers, she had her hands in his hair, her fingers combing deep into thick, wavy locks. Hers was a kiss of need, of a desperate yearning. A kiss of grief and also of hope.

His was a kiss she knew she'd never forget.

Forceful.

Passionate.

And all-consuming.

The tears and heartache faded away, replaced by a hunger to taste the pleasures he was promising. Greedily she clung to him, relishing the feel of his tongue probing her mouth, playing with hers.

Lying back down, he pushed the afghan aside and pulled her onto him, pressing her chest against his, aligning their hips. Her skirt hiked up to her thighs, and she felt his arousal and knew he wanted her. When his hand slid from her waist to her side, she turned so he could touch her.

Gentleness was not a necessity. To be taken, to be loved, cherished—those were the feelings she longed to experience. Inside, she ached, a void needing to be filled. Years of frustrated dreams cried for recognition.

Common sense was gone. Reason had vanished. Life was too short, too quickly crushed out. She didn't want to die never knowing the love of a man. She didn't want to go through life always being the friend, the buddy...the woman men joked with but never took to bed.

"Amy?"

The sound of her name made her shudder. Greg had moved his hand back to her side, had stopped kissing her. She didn't want him to stop.

"Amy," he repeated softly. "Not this way."

Please! she silently begged. *Love me. Please!*

He held her close, but she could feel the difference. He'd become the friend. She knew it before he even said anything. He would console her now, would tell her everything would be all right.

It wouldn't be.

She cried, her tears for the man who had died in her arms earlier that night, for the wife and children he'd left behind and for herself. She cried and she clung to Greg, and hated herself for wanting him, even for a short while. And when there were no more tears, she lay in the warmth of his embrace and wondered what to say next.

He solved the problem.

"Better?" he asked softly.

She felt like a fool.

"Better," she answered.

"Want to talk about it?"

Talk about how she'd just thrown herself at a man she barely knew? How she'd practically begged him to make love to her? "No," she said and pulled back. "I just want to go to bed. It's been a long night and I'm exhausted."

Embarrassed, she straightened her dress, her body still hot where he'd touched her, her lips bruised and her cheeks raw from the scrape of his beard. He said nothing when she stood, and she knew he was embarrassed, too. What had started as a friendly kiss of compassion had gotten out of hand. Her fault.

"I'm sorry," she apologized. "I..." She couldn't explain. "I'll see you tomorrow."

Turning away, she hurried from the room.

Chapter Nine

Greg stayed on the couch for a long time after Amy went up the stairs. In the quiet that surrounded him, he cursed his sanity, his libido and the miserable, stupid way he'd handled things. Here the woman had needed a shoulder to cry on, a chance to talk out her feelings. But no, he'd botched it up, started kissing her—wanting her. Another five minutes and they would have been making love.

He'd had to pull back, stop what he'd started. He'd had no choice. If she knew who he really was, she'd hate him.

She probably hated him anyway.

The next morning he woke before dawn but waited until he knew Amy was up and taking a shower before he got out of bed. He had a pot of coffee brewing and toast in the toaster by the time she came down the stairs. She was wearing navy slacks, a white blouse and her usual white work shoes. Over her arm she carried the white lab coat she would put on before going into the clinic. He noticed, even though she was wearing makeup, that her cheeks had the undeniable redness of whisker burns. Last night, Doc Amy had simply been a woman being kissed by a man.

Today?

The toast popped up, and she saw him, her expression a mixture of surprise and embarrassment. He smiled and tried to put her at ease. "Good morning. How do you feel today?"

"Rotten," she admitted. "What are you doing up so early?"

"Couldn't sleep."

She stopped in front of him. Her eyes were red-rimmed and puffy, and he knew she'd been doing a lot of crying. More than just the time in his arms. "Greg," she started. "About last night. I'm sorry... for the way I behaved."

He leaned on his crutches and reached out and touched her shoulders. "No need for an apology. I'm the one who should be saying I'm sorry. You were tired. Upset because a man had died. You needed someone to talk to, and what did I do? I started coming on to you."

"I..." She looked down at the linoleum between them. "Normally I don't..." There was a pause. "Well, act the way I did last night."

He'd suspected as much. "Hey, you'd had a rough night."

She kept staring at the linoleum. "I know how I look... how men feel about me."

Hooking a finger under her chin, he brought her face back up so she had to look at him. "And how do men feel about you?"

Her voice quavered just slightly. "They see me as a friend, but when it comes to...to more...well..." She took a deep breath and straightened, tilting her head back even more. "Your reaction last night was my fault. I'm a doctor. I know men get aroused easily. I also know when it comes to mak-

ing love, a man likes to wake up with a woman who has
smeared mascara, not a road-map on her face.''

Angry with her assumption, Greg pulled her close, nearly
toppling them both over. Only by wrapping his arms around
her was he able to keep his balance. ''Look here, *Dr.* Fraser,
who knows all about men, I did not stop what we were doing last night because you have scars on your face. Believe
me, the way I was feeling, that's the last thing that would
have bothered me. I stopped because I care about you. Because what I was doing was wrong.''

''Wrong?'' she scoffed. ''No. You know why you
stopped?'' She'd thought about it long enough through the
night. ''You stopped because you were afraid if you went
through with it, I'd make a big deal out of it today, expect . . . expect some kind of commitment.''

She was nearly in tears, but then, ever since Tom's death,
she'd felt that way. ''I . . . I just want you to know, I wouldn't
have expected anything. I wouldn't want a man to stay because he felt sorry for me.''

Amy wiggled to free herself, but he wasn't about to let her
go. Tightening his grip, he let the crutches fall away from his
sides. If he went, they both went.

Aluminum hit linoleum with a hollow ring. Greg concen-
trated solely on the woman in his arms. ''Amy, stop it! I am
not letting you go until we talk this out.''

''We've already talked,'' she insisted.

''No, you've told me what I've been thinking and feeling, and believe me, as a psychic, you're a flop.''

She stopped pulling back and looked at him.

''You are right. I stopped because I was afraid of how
you'd react later. The idea of making a commitment, however, wouldn't have stopped me. I've made love to women
without any commitment. What I do feel is necessary is
mutual respect and honesty.'' And he hadn't been honest

with her. "We barely know each other. You really don't know me at all."

Amy silently disagreed. Maybe it had been just a little more than forty-eight hours since they'd met, but she'd had a chance to see the compassion and kindness in him, feel the love he had to give and know the sharpness of his mind. Maybe Greg was keeping secrets from her—at least, she suspected as much—but on the other hand, in many ways she knew him better than Aaron, and people wanted her to marry Aaron.

"I stopped because I didn't want you hating me," Greg said. Hating him and herself.

"Why would I hate you?" The idea took her by surprise.

"Because I'm..." He stopped. Telling her who he was wouldn't make the situation better, and it could make it a lot worse. "Because I'm leaving today, and it would have seemed like I was taking advantage of the situation last night."

"I see," she said and looked away.

She didn't see, but it was the best he could come up with. "What I want to know is why you find it so unreasonable that a man might want to make love with you?"

"Because..." Still avoiding his eyes, she shrugged. "Because no man ever has."

He stared at her for a moment, uncertain what to say. In his arms was a warm, giving woman. He couldn't believe no man had seen beyond the surface. "Oh, Amy," he sighed, shaking his head. "Then they're the fools."

"I've always thought that." She looked at him, her laugh ragged and tense.

"If things were different..." He touched the side of her face. "If only you weren't a doctor."

"And what's my being a doctor have to do with this?"

He wasn't sure how to explain. "Honey, I spent my entire childhood in a stupor because of doctors—doctors and a woman who was so possessive she couldn't bear to let her child be a normal boy. That woman is dead now because doctors gave her what she asked for, not what she needed. To put it simply—and as you might have guessed—doctors are my least favorite people.''

''You're condemning an entire profession because of the mistakes of a few. Blaming me.'' Reaching up, she brushed the palm of her hand over the side of his beard, then slid her fingers into his hair. ''Greg, I'm an individual.''

A unique individual. Sweet, loving and vulnerable. For a moment he simply gazed into her eyes, then he groaned and lowered his mouth to hers.

It was at that exact second that the back door opened with a clamor and a squawk. Greg jerked his head back, and Amy pulled her hand away from his hair. Both of them looked toward the laundry area.

''Peggy!'' she gasped.

The older woman stood in the doorway—a suitcase in one hand, a bird cage in the other. Her sharp gaze held them captive, and Amy wasn't sure what to say. There was really no explaining away the situation. It was obvious Peggy had caught them about to kiss.

It seemed an eternity before the woman spoke. When she did, she kept her eyes on Greg. ''They're startin' work on my place. I'll be stayin' here f'r a while.''

''You're moving in?'' Amy glanced at the suitcase and the blue parakeet in its bird cage.

''I'll bring the rest of my things over later.''

''I'm leaving,'' Greg said, though he didn't move. He stood where he was, balanced on one foot, his arms around Amy.

Peggy smiled. ''Seems like I remember y'sayin' that yesterday... and th' day b'fore.''

Easing out of Greg's embrace, Amy knelt down and picked up his crutches, handing them up, one at a time.

Don't go, she silently willed. *Not yet.* Standing, she tried to come up with the right words. There was so much she wanted to say. All she could do was stare into his eyes. Those beautiful blue eyes.

"Don't you need to be opening up the clinic soon?" Peggy asked efficiently.

Amy knew the woman was trying to be helpful, trying to keep her from getting hurt, emotionally or physically. The closeness of a small town could be a bane or a benefit. At the moment, Peggy's interruption did not seem beneficial.

Touching Greg's arm, Amy made her plea. "Stay. At least until tomorrow. I don't make house calls on Saturdays. After I'm through in the clinic, I can drive you wherever you want to go."

He studied her face for a long time, saying nothing, then he glanced Peggy's way. When he looked back at Amy, he nodded.

The sun came out around two o'clock, long after Amy had left to make her house calls. Seated at the kitchen table, Greg watched the clouds break apart, slowly exposing larger and larger patches of blue. For most of the morning he'd read while Peggy cleaned the house. Going through the books on the shelves in the living room, he'd started with Melloni's *Illustrated Medical Dictionary* and ended with *The Making of a Woman Surgeon.* Mostly he skimmed pages, stopping whenever he came to something that related to his experiences. He wasn't sure any of it helped.

Earlier, Peggy had fixed soup and sandwiches for lunch. He had offered to help, to at least set the table, but she'd shooed him out of the kitchen, reminding him of the milk he'd spilled the day before. When Amy had come back from the clinic, Greg found no chance for a private talk with her. As soon as Amy sat down, Peggy had joined them and dominated the conversation.

The woman knew about their visits to Vern and Velma's and to Molly's. She also knew about the Cole boy stepping on a nail and had been there when Tom Gibson died. No communications system could be better than the one Peggy was tapped into.

"Sun's out," she said.

Greg looked away from the windows at the woman. He had a feeling Peggy had been waiting for Amy to leave so she could talk to him without fear of Amy's coming back and overhearing the conversation.

"Coming out, at least," he agreed.

"Thought you said nothin' was goin' on."

"Nothing is. Not the way you're thinking."

"And I suppose y'know how I'm thinkin'." She snorted. "You were supposed to be leavin' yesterday."

"I changed my mind."

"The longer y'stay, the harder it's goin' t'be on her."

"She asked me to stay," he reminded her.

Peggy studied him with her piercing brown eyes, then grunted. "Sometimes a woman don't know what's good f'r her. Just remember, I'm gonna be around from now on."

Greg decided to take advantage of the warm-up in the weather and get outside. Mostly he wanted to escape Peggy's watchful eyes. The woman was worse than a guard dog, and a couple of times he would have sworn he heard her growl.

Greg also wanted to see how it felt to walk with crutches for any distance. By the time he reached the downtown area, he knew. His arms ached, and the way he was walking was rubbing his armpits raw. Proceeding with his cross-country journey was out of the question...at least as long as he was on crutches.

The highway was the main street of Wyngate. Stores ranging from gun shops to video rentals stretched for five blocks on either side. There was only one signal and lots of parking. The town was as much like New York City as a drop of water was like the ocean.

Greg stopped and bought a soft drink at the grocery store. He'd no sooner stepped outside and popped open the can than a man in his late sixties wearing bib overalls stopped beside him. "You the feller livin' with Doc Amy?" he asked.

"I've been staying at her house for the last few days," Greg admitted. "But I'll be leaving soon. Tomorrow."

The man took a small round can from his pocket, pinched out a wad of tobacco and popped it into his mouth. Just when Greg thought the man had forgotten he was there, he continued. "She's got a young man, y'know."

"No, I didn't know that."

"Stone carver. He's away visiting his sister in Oregon."

The man offered Greg some tobacco from the can. Greg shook his head, and the man kept talking. "I hear Peggy's moved in with ya."

A woman going by overheard and stopped. Sternly she looked Greg up and down. "You the one Peggy's been telling me about?"

"I suppose." Greg could just imagine what Peggy had been saying. It was amazing the police hadn't stopped by to check him out.

"Says he's leavin' town tomorrow, Grace," the man chewing tobacco said. Grace nodded but kept studying Greg's face. "You look familiar."

"I've never been here before."

"You ever had your picture in the papers or anything like that?" She touched the tobacco chewer's arm. "John, you ever seen this man's picture before?"

Greg was sure he knew where Grace expected his photo to be—the post office's wanted posters.

"Hain't never seen him before," John answered and winked at Greg. "Grace here is our town librarian. She's got a photographic memory. Never forgets a face. Me, I'm lucky when I look in the mirror in the morning if I remember who *I* am."

Greg chuckled, but Grace kept staring at him. "I know I've seen you somewhere." She frowned. "Maybe without the beard."

Slowly her gaze moved over his hair, and Greg had a feeling Grace probably had seen his picture somewhere. Perhaps the profile a few years back in *People* magazine, or the article on him in *Time*. He just had to hope she didn't remember where, and go looking it up.

Quickly Greg finished his soda and tossed the empty can into the trash barrel near the curb. "Nice to have met you two," he said cordially and started down the sidewalk.

"You tell Doc Amy hello for me," John called after him.

"She has a boyfriend, you know," Grace added. "He'll be back soon."

Greg had a feeling that was a warning.

From the grocery store he went on to a clothing store. One thing he knew—he was going to need more shorts. With a cast on his leg, he wouldn't be wearing the jeans in his backpack. And he could use some new shoes. Well, at least one new shoe.

The moment he entered the store, a woman in her early twenties offered her help. Soon he had a pile of clothing and a pair of high-tops by the register. They weren't hiking shoes, but they would do until he reached a city that carried what he needed.

As she rang up his purchases, the woman kept looking at him, smiling coyly. Finally she spoke up. "I hear you're living with Doc Amy. That right?"

"I'm staying at her place." He rested his weight on his crutches and tapped his cast. "I was walking cross-country, but right now I can't do much with this ankle the way it is, so she said I could stay at her place for a few days."

"The woman's expression brightened. "So you don't know her that well?"

"I just met her the night I broke my ankle."

"That makes more sense." The woman nodded knowingly. "I mean, when I saw you come in here, right away I said to myself, 'What's a good-looking guy like him doing with someone like Doc Amy?'"

The woman's inference rankled Greg. "And what's wrong with Amy?"

"Well, nothing." She immediately changed her tone. "I mean, Doc Amy's the greatest. Absolutely the greatest."

"But?" Greg pried.

The woman shrugged. "Hey, you've seen her face. And the way she walks. She's a nice person. A really great doctor. I just don't see her with a guy like you."

"And what kind of a guy do you see her with?"

"Well, I guess the guy she's been dating. Aaron . . . the stone carver."

Greg was beginning to get tired of hearing about Aaron the stone carver. He was also beginning to feel just a little jealous. "So what's this Aaron like?"

"He's nice. Quiet. Might have been decent-looking, but he's got pockmarks all over his face and he's losing his hair." She looked at Greg's hair, then let her gaze slowly drop down over his body. When she looked back up, she grinned. "He's sure nothing like you, honey, but like I said, what can someone who looks like Doc Amy expect?"

"Anything she wants," he answered sharply. "You know, lady, beauty of the body is only half the fortune. And a pearl, though small, is better than a stone any day."

"Huh?" The woman stared blankly at him, and he decided it wasn't worth his time to explain what he meant. The moment she gave him his change, he took his bag of new clothes and shoes and left the store.

By the time he got back to the house, he knew there was no way he could continue his cross-country walk on crutches. He was also beginning to gain a new respect for the disabled and what they had to go through every day of their lives. Simply opening the back door and getting into the house was no easy feat. Exhausted, he dropped into the first chair he came to. Almost immediately he heard Peggy snort. "I see y're back."

"Just like a bad penny."

"Y'said it, not me." Peggy crossed in front of him and opened the refrigerator. "Dinner's at six."

Amy was tense all through dinner. While she'd been out making house calls, she'd made a decision. Maybe it was stupid and maybe she would fail, but she was going to try to convince Greg to stay. At least for a while. At least until she could put on a walking cast. Or maybe until his cast came off.

She didn't want to discuss her idea in front of Peggy, but as soon as the last bite of dinner was eaten, Amy began her campaign." Now that it's stopped raining, may I show you my backyard, Greg?"

He glanced out the windows.

It was obvious there wasn't all that much of a backyard to see, but there was the gazebo in the far corner, a place where two people could sit and talk. "Sure." He pushed his chair back and got up on his crutches.

Amy saw him wince as he settled on the armrests. "You okay."

"Just raw armpits. I think I overdid it this afternoon."

More fuel for her argument.

She took it slowly as she led him out the back door and onto her lawn. Her prize possession was a small limestone carving near the gazebo. Intricately detailed, the work showed a cat chasing a ball.

"It's a grave marker," she explained. "If you get up to Bedford, the Green Hill Cemetery has some fantastic limestone grave markers. Some look like tree trunks, with intricate carvings of vines and ropes twisting around them. They've been featured in articles and on TV. Not that this is from one of those graves. A friend carved this one for me after my cat got run over by a car. Mittens is buried right here."

"I think that was the cemetery I was supposed to go see, the one that took me off my course, got me lost and this ankle broken."

She laughed. "In that case, you really were lost. Bedford's miles from here."

Greg studied the cat. It was good. "Would this friend happen to be Aaron the stone carver?"

Amy glanced his way. "I forgot I'd told you about him."

"You and everyone in Wyngate. They've been warning me that you're already taken."

"Well, they're wrong. Aaron and I are simply friends."

Greg raised his eyebrows. "Does he know that?"

She nodded. "He did propose. I turned him down. That's one reason that he's in Oregon visiting his sister."

"Licking his wounds?"

"More like giving people around here a new view of our relationship. As I've said before, the problem with living in Wyngate is there's no privacy. The townspeople decided Aaron and I made a good couple and started pushing us together."

More than likely the townspeople decided Aaron was as good as Amy was going to get. If Amy had a handicap, it was this town. And that irritated Greg. "Dammit, Amy, you need to get away from this place. Go somewhere bigger, somewhere where everyone doesn't know everything you're doing."

"No." She didn't understand his anger. "I lived in a city like that. Chicago is certainly a place where no one knows what you're doing. I like living in Wyngate."

"Why? Because you feel protected here?" he scoffed. "These people aren't protecting you, they're smothering you."

She moved on to the gazebo. "You're exaggerating."

He followed her. "No, I'm not. The people of Wyngate have made up their minds as to who's right for you and who's not. Who you can get and who you can't get."

Stopping just inside the small, circular, lattice-sided structure, she turned and faced him. "You're saying they see Aaron as the best I can get?"

"Bingo." He wasn't trying to be cruel. He just wanted her to know what was happening.

"And what if I disagree with their opinion of who I can or cannot attract?"

"It doesn't matter. As I said, they've already made up their minds. Peggy's here, isn't she? You know why? She's here because she—and who knows how many others—feel I'm not right for you. Your housekeeper is here to watch over you. Protect you from me."

"You're wrong. Her house is being worked on," Amy argued. "I'd told her she could stay here long before you showed up."

"Maybe her house is being worked on, maybe it isn't. I don't know. I'm just telling you how it is. If you want to be protected and cared for, fine. But I think you deserve more than what they've got planned for you."

In part, Amy knew what he was saying was true. Only he seemed to be underestimating her. That, however, could be to her advantage. "You're saying I need to change the town's image of me?"

"That, or get out of this town." He'd opt for leaving.

"Would you be willing to help me?" she asked. "Actually, maybe we could help each other. You keep telling me you don't like doctors. Do you really know what it's like being a doctor?"

"What are you suggesting?" he asked cautiously.

"That you stay here for a while. It would give you a chance to see what being a doctor is like for me. The hours I keep. The kind of cases I get. In turn, your being here, living in my house, would certainly give the town a different image of me."

"I already know you keep terrible hours, and I have no desire to follow you around." But her idea wasn't out of the question. If he'd learned anything today, it was that he wasn't going to be going far on crutches. "How long are you suggesting I stay?"

"A week. Two. However long you want." She had a feeling she needed to make sure he knew he could leave, that she wasn't trying to hold him here. "In fact, there's a dinner a week from Saturday night to honor the doctors in Indiana's southern counties. If you went with me, you'd be surrounded by doctors. You could talk to them. Pick their brains, so to speak."

"And what are these doctors going to think when you show up at a dinner with a long-haired, bearded bum dressed in shorts?"

"That's the idea, isn't it? To shake up people's images of me? Besides, I think we could borrow a coat and tie for you, and I'll be glad to buy you a pair of slacks. We can cut one pant leg to go over your cast. You wouldn't look like a bum."

She was pretty sure he'd look great, and she knew none of the doctors would expect her to be with a man as good-looking as Greg. She doubted they expected her to be with any man. It would be fun to see their expressions. "There'd be no cost involved. Everything's being paid for by the Veterans of America.''

''I'd be your date.'' Greg said it as though he were trying out the idea.

''If you want to go.'' She could feel her cheeks growing warm and hoped it was dark enough in the shadows of the gazebo that he couldn't tell. ''If you don't want to go, you don't have to. I just thought it would give you a chance to mingle with doctors.''

Greg watched her bite her lower lip and nervously rub her hands up and down the sides of her slacks. His first impulse was to say no. For him to go to a doctors' banquet would be like throwing Daniel into the lions' den. Except he'd be the lion and they'd be the gladiators if they found out who he was.

On the other hand, he liked challenges, and it would be interesting to go to a dinner where he was surrounded by the enemy. ''Sure,'' he finally said. ''I'll go with you.''

''You will?'' Her eyes practically sparkled and the slow, surprised smile that took control of her mouth was as beautiful as a sunrise. ''So you'll stay for a while then? At least another week?''

''At least another week.'' He felt it would work. That was, as long as Amy and he weren't going to be the only ones living in the house. Alone with her . . .

''We'll even be quite proper,'' she said, grinning. ''After all, as you've pointed out, we do have our chaperon.''

He glanced back toward the house. Peggy was at the window, looking their way.

Amy laughed softly. ''She really is worried about you, even though I keep telling her you're harmless.''

''Ah, you are much too trusting, my dear. Don't you know what Leo says?''

She shook her head, and Greg winked. ''Leo says, 'Beware of the lion. Even an injured one can bite.' ''

Chapter Ten

The weekend went rather well, Amy thought, considering three totally unalike adults were living under the same roof—her roof. She did have some trouble keeping her pulse rate from jumping into the danger zone whenever Greg was near, but he seemed intent on not letting things get out of hand, as they nearly had the night Tom died. Greg was a toucher, though. At the most unexpected moments, he would casually place a hand on hers, give her nose a tweak, or brush her hair back from her face. There was no more kissing, however, and she did laugh at the way Peggy always seemed to appear whenever Greg came around.

He was right. It was obvious Peggy didn't approve of him. She constantly criticized his long hair and made digs about his not having a job. She also kept asking him questions about his past, which he deftly avoided answering, much to Amy's disappointment.

By Sunday night, however, Amy could tell Greg was winning Peggy over. The change started when he asked about her bird and got her to take the parakeet out of its cage. The laughter came when the bird decided Greg's tawny mane made a perfect nesting spot and settled down right on top of his head.

That was when Peggy said if Tweetie liked him, he couldn't be all bad.

Monday started off as a normal Monday, the clinic filled to capacity with walk-ins who over the weekend had suddenly developed aches and pains that, in their opinion, needed immediate attention. Amy was so glad they'd waited until Monday and not bothered her on Sunday, that she worked everyone in.

At one o'clock, Lisa, the nurse who kept the clinic running with maximum efficiency, announced the waiting room was empty and Amy was to call Barbara Bosker—something about the auction. Amy did, then wished she hadn't.

Barbara was moving. Barbara was also the woman who had said not to worry, said she'd take care of all the publicity for the auction. Amy was now worried.

She needed to talk about it—to someone—but when she went back into the house, Peggy informed her that Greg had gone out. "Who knows where," she said with a sniff and headed for the back door. "I've got t'be goin' myself. Th' Ladies' Aide is preparin' food f'r those who stop by after Tom Gibson's funeral." She paused to look back. "Y'll be at th' funeral, won't ya?"

"I'll be there," Amy said.

She ate her sandwich in the silence of the empty house, wondering where Greg had gone and just what she was going to do now that she didn't have Barbara. She didn't have an answer to either question by the time she grabbed her bag and left to make her house calls, then to attend Tom's funeral.

She was upset when she returned. Funerals always depressed her, this one especially. Tom Gibson had been so young, had had so much to live for. One mistake, and now he was dead.

What she'd learned at the funeral had also upset her. Greg Lyman had lied to her.

He was sitting at the kitchen table, peeling potatoes while Peggy fussed at the stove. Amy stopped at the doorway. "You," she called out, pointing a finger at him. "I want to see you in the clinic."

Peggy turned and looked her way. "Problem, Doc Amy?"

Yes, there was a problem. She'd been played for a sucker, and she didn't like it. "No, no problem," she fibbed. "I just want to check his cast."

Greg frowned. "Right now?"

"Yes." The word came out too sharply. She forced herself to smile. "While I still have the energy to play doctor."

He put down the potato he was peeling and got up on his crutches. She led the way, and he followed. As soon as they were in the clinic and she was sure Peggy couldn't hear, Amy turned to him. "You lied to me."

She knew a guilty look when she saw one, and Greg looked guilty as sin.

"It was the librarian who told you, wasn't it?" he said.

"No. Joanie Watkins."

Greg frowned, the name unfamiliar to him.

"The clerk at Max's. The clothing store in town," Amy explained. "I saw her at Tom Gibson's funeral today. I must have sounded like a real fool, telling her you were staying here because you didn't have any money. I think she really enjoyed letting me know you'd been in the store Friday and had paid for your purchases with hundred dollar bills."

Amy glared at him. "Then Crystal, one of the tellers at the bank, said you'd had some money wired to you this afternoon. Lots of money."

"So?" Greg still didn't understand what the problem was ... or if she knew who he was or not. Brian had simply wired the money to Gregory Lyman, as he'd asked him to do.

"So I feel like a fool," Amy sputtered. "You lied to me, telling me you couldn't afford to go to a hospital, that you were out of money and living on the streets."

"I never said I was out of money or living on the streets. Or that I couldn't afford to go to a hospital. I said I didn't *want* to go to a hospital. That's different."

"You said you couldn't pay me," she reminded him.

He tried to remember what he had said. That night had been a daze. "I think I asked what you'd do if I couldn't pay you."

"Same thing," she insisted.

He shook his head. "No. I wanted to know what you would do if someone who was injured came to you and couldn't pay you. You answered my question. Now, if it's your bill you're worried about, just tell me what I owe and I'll pay."

"I don't care about what you owe me," she snapped. "It's ... it's—"

Amy stopped herself. Actually, he was right. Other than his question about what she would do if he couldn't pay, he hadn't said he didn't have any money. That night she'd assumed he was one of the many homeless living off the streets. She'd made an assumption based on his appearance. Jumped to a conclusion.

An erroneous conclusion, evidently. And now she was making a fool of herself. All because it scared her to know he did have money, to realize he could leave—go to California—whenever he wanted. "And what would you have done if I'd said I wouldn't treat you if you didn't have any money?"

"That night, I would have paid you." He smiled. "But you didn't say that, did you?"

"No, I didn't." She guessed, as leery as he was of doctors, she should be pleased she'd passed his test. Today she wasn't sure how she felt. "I'm sorry for yelling at you just now. It's been one of those days." She turned away, going into the nearest examining room. "Come on, as long as you're here, let me check that cast."

"And what's gone wrong today?" he asked, following her into the room.

"Everything." She patted the table, and he pulled himself up on it. "Mondays are always miserable. If I were smart, I'd leave town on Mondays. No, if I were smart, I'd forget trying to keep this clinic open, do as you said and get out of this town, let the people around here drive to Bedford."

"What happened this Monday to turn you so sour on the people of Wyngate?"

"The people?" She looked up from his cast. "It's not the people. It's Barbara Bosker. My dearest friend. Barbara, who promised she'd take care of all the publicity for this auction next month. Who promised I wouldn't have to worry about a thing. Barbara, who has now suddenly decided to move to Denver."

Amy tested his cast for looseness. "Your foot doesn't look swollen, but the cast still feels fairly snug. Any itching?"

"Some, but I can live with it." He was more interested in knowing more about what had made her so upset. "When is this Barbara moving?"

"Next week." Amy checked around the edges of the cast for signs of chafing or infection. "When she called today, she had the gall to tell me she was sorry, but she hasn't had time to make any posters or send out any news releases, but could I work her in this week for a complete exam. She doesn't know what she's going to do without me." Amy sighed. "Maybe I can get some kids to make the posters."

"How about if I make them?"

She looked up from his leg. "You?"

"With me staying until at least next weekend, it would give me something to do during the day. Keep me out of mischief." He grinned. "Keep Peggy from harping on me about how I'm sponging off you."

"You don't need to feel you have to do anything." She felt like a heel. He wasn't sponging off her; she wanted him around. "I shouldn't have snapped at you earlier. I'll talk to Peggy."

"No." Greg touched her hand. "Amy, I'd be glad to make some posters for you. Heck, I'll even help you with the news releases. I'm already sick of sitting around and watching television. It would be good for me."

She considered the idea. She could understand Greg's need to be doing something, and his offer would certainly help. "I don't want you to feel you have to do this, or that you owe me anything."

"Ah, but I do." He squeezed her fingers. "So now, tell me, what do you want these posters to say?"

They discussed the publicity that would be necessary to get word of the auction beyond the local area. Time was forgotten, until Peggy came back to check on them. If the woman expected to catch them in a compromising position, she was disappointed. When she walked into the room, Greg was still on the examining table, jotting ideas down on the back of a prescription pad, and Amy was sitting in the chair in the corner, too amazed by the way he was taking over to do much more than answer his questions.

Peggy simply announced that dinner was ready.

Tuesday morning, Greg called around until he found a store that carried art supplies. By Tuesday afternoon, twenty sheets of poster board, an assortment of soft lead pencils, several bottles of waterproof ink, brushes, pens and color markers were special-delivered to Dr. Amy Fraser's house. Greg started work immediately.

For him, a poster wasn't that different from what he'd been doing for the past ten years. Coming up with publicity releases and places to send them was more difficult.

Timing would be everything. He had to get the articles into the papers far enough ahead of the auction that people would plan on attending, and close enough that they wouldn't forget.

On the posters, he used a caricature of a parakeet, an amazingly few lines giving the image of a cockeyed bird delivering a simple message—Good Health is a Community Affair. Peggy loved the crazy bird. Amy liked the directness of the statement. It was what she believed.

By Friday he had the press releases ready to go and a list of papers to send them to. After he was gone, Amy could put them in the mail by the dates he'd determined they'd do the most good.

Saturday, from the moment Amy finished in the clinic until it was time to leave for the banquet, everything seemed to focus on getting dressed. Greg had bought a suit, paying for it himself. Joanie Watkins had gladly helped him go through the sparse selection at Max's, then she'd carefully opened the seam on the right pant leg so he could get the trousers over his cast. Unlike Amy, Joanie hadn't blushed when she saw him in his briefs. What she did do was keep making suggestions that she was available if he was interested.

He wasn't.

By the time Amy came down the stairs, Greg was dressed and waiting. He'd carefully trimmed his beard and pulled his mane back into a ponytail. The suit he'd picked out was a conservative blue pinstripe and not a bad fit for being store bought off the rack. Even Peggy approved.

"Y'look almost civilized," she said, scrutinizing him from the top of his head to the shine of his one black shoe.

"The picture of a true gentleman, right?"

"More like a wolf in sheep's clothing," she scoffed.

Amy came down the stairs slowly. It was the second time Greg had seen her in a dress, and this one was definitely sexier than the first one, the soft blue material clinging to her body, caressing her breasts and hugging her waist before flaring out to fall just above her knees. She wore flats, as always, and her steps down the staircase were awkward, but Greg thought she looked perfect.

She stopped at the bottom of the stairs and stared at him. He couldn't pull his gaze away from her. She'd done something to her hair, fluffed it out so it had more body. And she'd put on dangling silver earrings and used a muted blue eye makeup that made her eyes seem even larger than ever. Greener.

"You look great," she said, and nervously licked her lips.

Greg wanted to close the distance between them, wanted to touch her, see if she'd feel as soft as she looked, if she'd respond to a kiss as willingly as her eyes said she would. For one brief moment, he wanted to forget a dinner for doctors, his broken ankle and reason, wanted to carry her off to a place where they would be alone, kiss her until she moaned out his name, then slowly strip away her soft, sexy, blue dress and discover the woman beneath.

"Y'look lovely," Peggy said and stepped between them. "That dress . . ."

Over and over, the woman repeated the same phrases, clucking as she subtly tried to straighten the dress's low neckline so it showed less cleavage. A tinge of pink touching her cheeks, Amy looked to Greg for help.

He read her signal. "Are you ready?" he asked. "We don't want to be late."

While Peggy continued to hover nearby, Amy found her purse and car keys, and Greg waited by the back door. It wasn't until they were in the car and headed for Bedford that he said what he'd wanted to say earlier "You look beautiful. Sexy."

"Thank you." Amy kept her attention on her driving, but he saw the color again creep into her face. "I don't usually wear anything like this, but I decided, since we're trying to change my image..." She shot him a quick look. "It's not cut too low, is it? I don't want to embarrass you."

"Embarrass me?" He chuckled and reached over, touching the skirt of her dress, feeling the softness of the fabric and the warmth of her thigh. Gently he gave her leg a squeeze. "Honey, I can't imagine anything you could ever do that would embarrass me. And no, it's not cut too low. Although, for a moment when you came down the stairs, I did think of grabbing you and denning up with you for a few hours of pure sex."

She glanced his way, her eyes filled with curious disbelief, then she looked back at the road. He watched her take in a deep breath and slowly release it. Her smile was more confident. "I think tonight's going to be fun."

He prayed she'd still feel that way by the end of the evening, that he didn't say or do anything that would embarrass *her*... that no one recognized him.

The temperature outside was warm, even at seven, but the banquet room at the Stonehenge Lodge was air-conditioned. Amy was sure the men in their suit jackets appreciated the coolness, but it wasn't long before she wished for sleeves and a higher neckline. Standing near the bar that had been set up, sipping from the glass of wine Greg had bought her, she shivered. Immediately he slipped an arm around her shoulders, bringing her close to his side and the warmth of his body. The next shiver that ran down her spine had nothing to do with the temperature in the room.

Doctors from miles around were in attendance, mostly men accompanied by their wives or girlfriends. There was one other woman doctor. Sarah Murphy. Sarah was with her husband, Joe, who was also a doctor and her partner, and soon the two came over to Amy. Sarah wanted to tell her about their new office.

Amy barely listened. She was more aware of Greg, of the rough, warm feel of his jacket against her skin, and of the scent of lime from the cologne he'd used. She watched him glance around the room, his nostrils slightly flared, as if sniffing for danger. He looked tame wearing a suit and tie, yet she could feel the tension in his body. Like a wild animal, he was poised and ready for danger.

Sarah and Joe began talking about patients, and Amy suddenly realized bringing Greg to this banquet might have been a mistake. She'd wanted to prove hers was a noble profession, to change his mind about doctors—about her. Joe and Sarah weren't going to help.

They were telling stories about medical school, when they were both interning at the same hospital. There, Joe bragged, they'd made love in a bed next to a woman in a coma. "I've always wondered, when she came out of the coma, if she remembered what we did." Sarah laughed. "Actually, I'm surprised I had the energy to make love. What I remember most about those years was how little sleep I got, and the mistakes I made. I still remember the time I prescribed the wrong medicine for a patient and—"

"Sarah..." Amy couldn't let her go on. She'd felt Greg's body tense. She was proving something all right. She was proving he was right. "...you're making us sound like a bunch of sex-crazed incompetents. Why brag about the mistakes? Why not talk about the people you've saved?"

Sarah looked at her in surprise. "Amy, you know how it was. How it is. My gosh, looking back, I don't see how we made it through those years. Then, if I hadn't had Joe or looked at the funny side of things, I think I would have gone crazy. I still feel that way, especially when someone comes to me, and I haven't the slightest idea what's wrong, I just know they're dying. Half the time I don't think doctors have the slightest idea what they're doing."

"But dammit, you should know!" Greg growled.

"We're not perfect." Sarah stepped back, closer to her husband. "Maybe patients think we know it all, or wish we did, but we don't. Neither Joe nor I have the time to read all the new studies in the medical journals. And even if we did, there's always the case you've never seen before, the symptoms that don't fit the pattern. Or the critical information the patient doesn't tell us."

"Some even outright lie," Joe added. "That always amazes me. Here I'm trying to help them, and they're playing games."

"Dinner is served," the head waiter announced. Joe and Sarah used the call as an excuse to hurry off.

"Sorry," Greg murmured, and Amy looked up. His mouth a tight line, he was staring at Sarah's back.

"I almost blew it," he said.

"You want to leave?"

He glanced down at her, and she watched his features soften into a smile. "No. Actually, this is very interesting."

Together they went to their table, Greg awkwardly maneuvering on his crutches as he moved between chairs, Amy limping by his side. They were seated with a new group, the woman next to Greg fascinated by his long hair. When he told her he'd been hiking cross-country, she peppered him with questions. The others were more interested in discussing golf games. Since she didn't play golf, Amy tried to relax and simply listen, but that was impossible. All through the meal she worried about what Greg was thinking and feeling. If he would leave in the morning.

How she would survive when he did leave.

When the master of ceremonies stood and began his humorous monologue on the trials and tribulations of being a country doctor, Greg pushed his chair close to hers and snaked an arm around her back. She looked at him, and he grinned and winked, nodding toward the front of the room, where the man continued his routine. She tried to listen, but the moment Greg's fingertips began making circles on her bare arm, she gave up the effort. Breathing became more important, remembering to take in a breath . . . then to let it out. He was beginning to relax; she wasn't. Playfully he blew into her ear, the warmth of his breath heating her blood and turning her insides liquid. She nearly groaned, then remembered where they were.

She was sure it was all a game to him, innocent flirtation. His effort to change her image. He'd never know how good he made her feel, how normal. Long after he was gone she would remember this night.

He continued to tease her on the drive home, tracing a fingertip over her exposed knee, then slowly moving it and her dress up her thigh until she slapped his hand and told him to behave himself. He grumbled good-naturedly and attacked a new area, the backs of his fingers climbing up the side of her neck to brush against her ear. "Did you have a good time?" he asked.

"I had a wonderful time. And you?"

Greg slipped his hand behind her neck. "Actually, I found the evening rather amusing."

She glanced his way. "You seemed quite tense most of the time."

"I was. But probably not for the reasons you think." It was time to tell her, he decided. No more excuses. They were only a block from the clinic, and even if she kicked him out of the car, he wouldn't have far to go before he could get his things. She deserved the truth. "Amy, there's something you should know . . ."

He hesitated, and she broke in. "What I know is tonight has been the happiest night of my life." She slowed the car and looked at him. "Tonight, Greg, you made me feel beautiful."

He decided what he had to say could wait until morning.

Chapter Eleven

Sunday, Greg didn't have a chance to tell Amy. In the morning, Peggy insisted they all go to church. In the afternoon, Amy was called out on an emergency. She didn't get back until late and looked too tired to cope with anything.

Monday, Greg decided. Monday he would tell Amy who he was, then he would leave.

Monday the X-ray machine stopped working.

"It's dead. Kaput. Finished," Amy said, slumping into a chair at the kitchen table. "I might as well give it up, close this clinic and go job hunting."

"You can't leave us," Peggy cried. Desperately she looked at Greg, though he had no idea what to do. He'd give her the money for a new X-ray machine if he could, but the bulk of his money was tied up in securities. It wasn't as if he could call Brian and have one or two hundred thousand sent to Wyngate, Indiana.

"So, you need a little more money than you'd figured," he said. "Maybe if I beef up those press releases, get the word out about the situation..." He wasn't sure it would work, but he was willing to give it a try for her sake.

"You'll stay and do that for me?" she asked, some life coming back into her eyes.

"Sure. What else have I got to do?" He lifted a crutch. "Even after I get off these, I'm not going to be able to walk any great distances."

That afternoon he revised the press releases he'd written. Tuesday he sent them out. They received varying responses. Wyngate's small weekly paper did a nice article explaining that not only did the town need to come up with enough money to keep the clinic open, but now they needed to raise money for a new X-ray machine.

The Bedford *Times-Mail* had a small article on Amy's hopes of keeping the clinic open after funding from the hospital ran out, but how lack of an X-ray machine would probably end those hopes. The Indianapolis *Star,* on the other hand, called and did an expanded article, focusing more on Amy and her old-fashioned method of making house calls than on the auction or the need for an X-ray machine.

It was that article that brought a surprise telephone call. And when Greg hung up, he was sure Amy wasn't going to have any problems finding the money to keep her clinic going or to get her X-ray machine. He could hardly wait until she got back from making her house calls.

"Guess who called," he said the moment she walked through the door.

"Who?" She set her bag down, grinning at his enthusiastic welcome.

"Opal Robinson. Or at least her producer. Opal wants you to be on her show. She saw the article about you in the *Star.* It's your practice of making house calls that interests her, but you can also pitch the auction and your need for a new X-ray machine. Your problems are over, gal."

Except she didn't look like her problems had ended. The smile that had brightened her face disappeared. Her shoulders slumped, and she shook her head. "You'll have to tell them thanks, but I can't do it."

"Can't do it?" It wasn't the answer he'd expected, nor had he expected Amy to look as if he'd just issued a death sentence. Confused, Greg swung over on his crutches to stand in front of her.

Even Peggy stopped shredding lettuce to stare at Amy. "Why not?" she asked.

"Because . . . because I just can't."

Amy tried moving past him, but he reached out and caught her arm. "You don't understand. This is a perfect opportunity. You'd be on national television. Millions of people would see you, hear your story. After that show aired, I bet you wouldn't be able to keep track of the items you'd get for your auction and the money people would send."

"I can't do it," she repeated firmly, looking at his knees, not his face.

It was his turn to ask, "Why not?"

"It certainly would be a thrill to see you on that show," Peggy said from across the room. "Why, I bet everyone in Wyngate would watch."

Amy looked at Peggy, then back at Greg. He saw the determination in her eyes, the resolve in her stiff posture. "I'm not going to do it," she repeated. "And that's that. Now, I don't want to hear any more about it."

She pulled loose from his grasp and limped out of the room. Peggy looked his way, but he didn't have any answers. He did know that besides determination, he'd seen fear in Amy's eyes. And pain.

Amy was glad Greg didn't bring up the subject of the Opal Robinson show during dinner, but it put a strain on the conversation. Both Peggy and Greg kept watching her, as though waiting for her to explain.

She didn't.

As soon as dinner was over, she made an excuse and disappeared into the clinic. There she went over her accounts, hoping that balancing credits and debits would keep her from thinking about the opportunity of a lifetime that she'd just turned down. By ten o'clock she'd not only balanced her books, she'd ordered all of the supplies she would need for the next month and was busily cleaning the supply cabinet. The only thing she hadn't done was vanquish the memory of Greg's questioning look when she'd said no.

Her concentration broke at the sound of the door from the house to the clinic opening. A box of latex gloves in her hand, she stepped to the doorway and watched Greg come down the hallway, the tap of his crutches a steady, forceful rhythm.

His mouth was a straight, unsmiling line, his gaze focused on her face. He stopped directly in front of her, his nostrils slightly flared from his exertion. Looking down at her, he repeated his one question. "Why not?"

Turning away, she stepped back into the storeroom and finished putting the box on the shelf. "I told you, I don't want to talk about it."

"Well, I do."

He followed her into the cramped area, and she realized she'd made a mistake. A room with barely enough space for one person to turn around in was not a good arena for an argument. Especially not an argument with a man whose nearness left her unstable under the best of circumstances.

"Greg, please," she pleaded, backing up slightly to give herself a little more room.

"Please, what?" He closed the space between them, pressing her against the shelving. "Please don't ask for reasons? Forget it, honey. When someone turns down a golden opportunity, I want to know why. I want to know what you're afraid of, Amy.''

"I'm not afraid of anything," she lied. "I just don't want to do it."

"Give me one good reason."

"I...I..." She squeezed her eyes tightly closed and drew into herself. "I just can't do it."

"Amy." She heard his crutches hit against the shelving, then felt sinewy-strong arms wrap around her. He drew her to his warmth and softly breathed his plea into her ear. "Talk to me, honey. Tell me what it is."

With most people, she kept up a facade. Amy Fraser, the invincible. Doc Amy, the care giver who didn't care what she looked like. For nearly two decades her theory had been if you didn't let anyone know it hurt, it wouldn't hurt. Only it always had. In Greg's arms, she felt the armor slipping. A shudder vibrated through her body, and she gave in.

"You're going to say I'm just feeling sorry for myself, that I'm wrong, but I can't stand the idea of millions of people seeing my...my..."

She couldn't say it.

"Your face?" he finished for her.

"My scars. Greg, maybe you don't think I look bad, but I know differently. Ever since the accident, I've had people staring and pointing at me. Children come right out and ask how I got the lines on my face. Actually, that doesn't bother me as much as the people who try not to notice, try not to say anything and go away feeling sorry for me. The point is, I do not want to go on the Opal Robinson show and be seen as a freak."

"You are not a freak, Amy. What can I say to convince you that your face does not look that bad?"

"Nothing." She'd seen herself in too many mirrors. "Look, I know what I look like. And I've seen talk shows where the guest is disfigured and everyone feels so very, very sorry for him or her. I don't want to be in that position."

"It wouldn't be like that," he argued, but she could tell she'd started him thinking. Slowly he loosened his hold, and finally he sighed. "Okay, I'll call them tomorrow and tell them you can't do it."

"Thank you, Greg."

Gently he brushed his fingertips over her cheek. "You're wrong, though. You're not someone people would feel sorry for."

With the smooth pad of his thumb, he traced the contour of her lips, and shivers raced down her back.

"You have a beautiful mouth."

And he had the softest, sexiest, most soothing purr of a voice.

"Beautiful eyes."

He leaned close, blew her bangs away from her eyes and brushed a kiss against her forehead. She was the one who purred.

"Personally," he said, "I think you have a beautiful face."

She laughed lightly. "I think maybe I'd better check your eyes tomorrow. You seem to be having some problems with your vision."

"My vision's just fine," he murmured. Snuggling her closer, he cradled her in his arms. Eyes open, he lowered his mouth to hers.

Greg lay on his bed in the dark, staring at the ceiling, mentally kicking himself for being so damned insensitive. He should have realized Amy wouldn't want to go on television. Ever since he'd met her, he'd seen how the scars on her face bothered her. But did he think about that? No. Here he'd thought he was helping her. All he'd done was hurt her.

A soft knock at his door made him start. Amy had gone upstairs over an hour ago and for the past ten minutes, he'd heard Peggy's snores from the next room. The woman was still snoring.

"Yes?" he called out.

The door opened slowly, the light in the hallway silhouetting Amy's figure. She was wearing the fluffy gold robe she'd let him borrow that first night, her honey-touched hair was tousled and her feet were bare. "I wasn't sure if you'd still be awake," she whispered.

"I'm awake. Come on in." He pulled himself to a sitting position, drawing the sheet to his waist. Beneath it, nothing more than a pair of skimpy blue nylon briefs and the cast on his leg covered his body.

He reached over to switch on the lamp on the nightstand, but Amy saw what he was doing. "Don't turn it on," she said quickly, then added, "If you don't mind."

"Sure." Sitting back, he watched her, waiting for her to make the next move. With the light at her back, her face was merely a shadow.

"Can we talk?" she asked hesitantly.

"Of course. Do you want me to get dressed and meet you out there?"

"No." She stepped into the room, closing the door behind her. For a moment she stood where she was, accustoming her eyes to the darkness of the room, the only sounds her breathing and his, then she moved forward, her bare feet scarcely making a rustle over the carpeting.

His eyes were already accustomed to the dark, and he followed her progress. Midway to his bed, she stopped. "I think Peggy's asleep," she whispered.

The sound of a snore from the other side of the wall was answer enough. Greg chuckled. "Your chaperon is off duty." He patted the edge of the bed and scooted to the side to make room. "Come on over and sit down, said the lion to the lamb."

Amy laughed nervously. "Sometimes you do remind me of a lion." She came to the edge of the bed, but continued to stand. "Am I wrong, Greg? Am I being totally self-centered in refusing to go on Opal's show?"

He said nothing and she went on. "For the last hour I've been thinking about it. For some of the people around here, it won't matter if this clinic closes. They'll go to Bedford. They'll find other doctors, other clinics. But for some of these people, I'm important. Other doctors won't go to their homes, won't take the time to find out what's really bothering them. I came here because I felt I could help these people, could make a difference in their lives. Now..."

Greg waited, her shallow breathing the only sound in the room. Finally, she finished. "I don't know what to do."

"I think you should give yourself a day or two to think about it," he said. "If it's going to bother you too much, we'll find other ways to raise the money. On the other hand..."

Greg reached for her hand, and his fingers wrapped around her slender wrist. "You're not a freak, honey."

He pulled her down, so she had to sit on the edge of the bed. He could tell she didn't feel comfortable. Her wrist still his captive, she tried one-handed to pull her robe closed, but he could see a bit of the pale-colored nightshirt she wore.

He didn't feel comfortable, either, the thought of how little she had on beneath that robe arousing him. He placed his free hand over the part of her robe that covered her leg. Beneath the soft fabric, he could feel the solid warmth of her thigh. His hand moved higher. "What you are is a very desirable woman."

"Greg." She sucked in a breath. "I, ah..." Amy placed a hand over his, stopping his fingers from roaming farther. Self-consciously, she laughed, and he knew she was blushing. "I guess I shouldn't have come here, to your bedroom. Especially this late. I just never think of a man wanting to do anything with me."

"Well, honey, I'm here to work on that little misconception of yours."

She laughed again, the sound more natural. "That little misconception didn't just happen. You're talking to a woman who's lived through years of rejections."

"Who's rejected you?"

"Gobs of boys . . . men."

"Specifics. What boys? What men?"

For a moment he didn't think she'd answer, then, with a sigh, she told him. "All of the boys in the eighth grade after I got out of the hospital and came back to school. Not that I blame them. My face was a lot worse then."

Maybe she didn't blame them, but Greg knew it had hurt. She would have been around thirteen then, at an impressionable age. "And later?"

"High school was terrible, but later it got so men at least didn't turn away when they saw me. They never asked me out, however. Or, if they did, it was just as a friend."

"So over the years you've assumed you're not sexually attractive."

"What else should I assume?" She patted his hand on her thigh. "Oh, once there was a man who wanted to take me to bed. He was what you would call 'blind' drunk."

"Not funny," Greg said sternly.

"I know," Amy agreed. "I know."

"I'm not blind." Reaching over, he snapped on the light. Amy blinked at the brightness and tensed. Gently Greg stroked her face, one fingertip following the pale white path of a scar. "I see them, honey. I also see a very beautiful woman. A woman who cares for others, who's willing to give of herself. A woman with love to give."

She smiled ruefully. "And no one to give it to."

"Someone will come."

Amy reached out and touched his face, running her hand over his beard, then combing her fingers into his thick mane of hair. Maybe it was crazy. She barely knew him, but she wished that someone were him. "Kiss me, please," she begged.

He knew he shouldn't. She needed a man who would love and cherish her for the rest of her life. He couldn't do that. He also knew he should tell her who he was. Should tell her right now. Gazing into her eyes, he knew he couldn't do that, either. Not tonight. No woman he'd ever known had touched him as deeply as this one, had made him forget all sensibility.

He wrapped his arms around the fluffy bulk of her shoulders, bringing her closer. "This is crazy, you know," he sighed. "Crazy and wrong."

But he couldn't seem to stop himself.

Beneath the robe, he could feel her soft curves. His mouth touched hers, and he knew vintage wine could not be more intoxicating than the taste of her lips. He wanted to drink in all she was offering, make love to her—with her.

Afterward he would tell her who he was.

Afterward he would suffer the consequences.

For now, he couldn't get enough of her, his kisses growing in intensity. Like the serpent of temptation, his tongue slithered in, teasing and promising. His hands traveled to new places, sliding under her robe, finding the edge of her nightshirt, then soft, warm skin. Her breathing became as ragged as his, her body smelling lusciously feminine. Even as he held her, she held him close, her fingers moving from his hair to his back.

Fears and self-doubts forgotten, she gave as she received—eagerly and openly—her kisses honest and wild. She was the kitten, playful and impatient. The lioness, offering sheer pleasure. A shift of position, and the bed creaked. She held her breath as he opened her robe.

Huggable.

The word was blazoned in white across the front of her yellow nightshirt, pressed enticingly forward by her breasts. ''Very definitely,'' he said and hugged her.

His kisses landed on her neck and her shoulders, his beard brushing against the cotton of her nightshirt. He felt her tremble with anticipation and knew she was holding her breath, waiting for him to touch her. Gently he did, feeling the soft curve of a breast and the hard nub of a nipple.

''You feel so good,'' he murmured and heard her sigh.

The knock at his door jarred both of them, the sound ricocheting through the room. Greg jerked his hand back, and Amy stiffened. Both of them stared at the closed door.

''Yes?'' he asked cautiously.

Chapter Twelve

"You all right?" Peggy asked from the other side of the door. "I thought I heard you talking and the bed moving."

"I'm all right," Greg answered, his voice husky.

Amy held her breath. She felt like a kid caught by the teacher while sneaking kisses in the play yard.

"You're sure you're all right?" Peggy repeated. "I see your light's on."

"I had a dream. It woke me. Sorry to have bothered you." He looked at Amy and grimaced.

Peggy persisted. "It's just that I'm a light sleeper, and when I heard noises over here, I got worried."

Amy also grimaced. Peggy's message was clear. The woman knew exactly what was going on...and had decided it was time to stop it. Her self-appointed chaperon had stepped in.

"Everything's fine. Nothing to worry about," Greg insisted. Without making a sound, he pulled Amy's robe back up over her shoulders.

"If you're sure." Amy could hear the hesitancy in Peggy's voice. "Remember, I'm just in the next room."

"I'll remember, but nothing's going to happen."

That was obvious, now. Greg chuckled under his breath, and gave Amy's hand a squeeze. "Some things are not to be," he whispered.

"Tell me about it," she grumbled in frustration. Standing, she straightened her robe, tightening the sash.

"You all right?" he asked softly.

"Fine," she lied. How could she be all right when her body ached with a need only crawling into bed with Greg would satisfy? Life wasn't fair.

A couple of bumps and thumps from the other side of the wall told them Peggy was back in her bedroom. Greg motioned with his hand for her to go, and Amy glanced toward the door. She could stay if she wanted. A twenty-nine—no, nearly thirty-year-old woman shouldn't have to sneak out of a bedroom in her own house.

Yet she knew she would go. She did value her morals and what others thought of her. For a moment she'd simply forgotten everything except how much she wanted Greg. How much she cared for him, loved him.

That realization alone scared her. She loved Gregory Lyman, and he was going to leave. Maybe not tonight, but some day soon. He cared for her, but he didn't love her.

And she'd nearly given herself to him.

Amy looked back at Greg. "Go," he mouthed silently, again waving his hand toward the door.

As quietly as she could, she left his room.

Greg watched the door close behind her, then shut his eyes. He didn't know whether to curse Peggy or bless her. The way things were going, another five minutes and he would have been making love with Amy. Even now he wanted her—physically and emotionally—and that scared him. He was starting to care too much, was feeling things he didn't want to feel. Somehow Amy had gotten under his protective veneer.

In the morning, Amy did what she could to cover the whisker burns on her face and greeted Peggy as though nothing had happened. She wasn't sure how she'd react when she saw Greg, but she didn't need to worry. He didn't get up for breakfast.

"He had a rough night," Peggy said. "I heard him tossing and turning until early this morning."

Peggy's raised eyebrows said volumes, but Amy kept her answer vague. "Probably that cast. I remember when my leg was in a cast, I could never find a comfortable position."

"Probably a stiff muscle," Peggy said, then chuckled.

Amy nearly choked on her orange juice.

She did see Greg that afternoon. He looked uneasy and the moment Peggy left them alone, he spoke up. "I have something to tell you."

He was going. She could tell. He was about to tell her what had happened the night before had been a mistake. He would thank her for all she'd done, then he would leave.

She didn't want him to leave. Not yet. "Greg, I need you here. I can't do the publicity like you've been doing. No one around this town could. And if I go on the Opal Robinson show..."

"You've decided to do it?"

"I'm thinking about it."

"Oh, Amy."

She was making life difficult for him. Greg knew he should tell her who he was. He should have told her days ago. Weeks ago. He should leave. The night before they'd nearly made love.

But she wanted him to stay.

Needed him to stay.

His thoughts were going in circles. They had been all night. He'd thought he'd come to the right decision, that he would tell her who he was and go with whatever happened.

"I need you to tell me I can do it," she said softly, a hint of all her insecurities creeping into her voice.

Maybe that was more important than who he was, he decided. Casually he slid his arm around her shoulders. "You can do it. So do I call them?"

"Ah..." Amy leaned against him and offered a silent prayer of thanks. He would stay. At least for a while longer. Now all she had to do was convince herself that she could go in front of a camera. "Give me until tomorrow."

The next morning, Grace Danville came to the clinic to have a stiff elbow checked. By the time Grace left, Amy had a feeling there'd never been anything wrong with the elbow, that Grace had merely wanted to see her expression when she told Amy what she'd learned about her houseguest.

As soon as the last patient was cared for, Amy went looking for Greg. She found him in the kitchen, working on the flyers he wanted printed and distributed. Again he was using a caricature of a parakeet as the main focus. Amy wondered why it had taken Grace to point out the obvious. The deceptively simple lines of the bird should have told her. Its cocky stance. Its saucy boldness. For years she'd seen that same style of drawing. Had loved it.

She stopped beside the table. "I want to talk to you. Alone."

Amy knew her voice sounded sharp. Greg looked up from the drawing and frowned. Peggy was putting soap in the washing machine in the laundry area. She called into Amy. "I'm leaving in a minute. I'm goin' t'check on how they're coming with my house."

"Thanks." Amy's gaze stayed on Greg. He looked unsure of what was up and that pleased her.

Capping his pen, he laid it down and got up on his crutches. He was standing by her side when Peggy pulled the back door closed behind her. "What's up, Amy?"

"The deception, that's what's up, Mr. G. M. Lyon."

She watched his eyes. He understood immediately. At first he started to say something, then he closed his mouth and expelled a long breath. Finally he did speak. "I was going to tell you."

"Well, now you don't need to. Grace Danville, our town librarian, did. She came in to see me this morning. She said she knew she'd seen your face somewhere, but it was almost by accident that she came across a photo of you in an old issue of *People* magazine. She brought the magazine with her, so I could see it for myself. Of course you didn't have a beard in the picture, but your hair looked the same."

And his eyes. Those beautiful blue eyes that seemed able to mesmerize her so easily.

Except the picture in the magazine had been in black and white, and the look in his eyes then had been amused, as if he'd just told or heard a very funny joke. The look in his eyes should be amused now. He'd certainly played a joke on her.

"From the very beginning, you've lied to me. Played me for a fool." And she hated him for that.

"What should I have told you that first night, Amy? Hey, Doc, you know that cartoonist who's been lambasting the medical profession for the past year, well, here I am?"

"Yes!" she cried, her anger overriding the emotions she didn't want to acknowledge. "If not that first night, the next day. How could you not tell me? I took you into my house. My home." *Nearly climbed into bed with you.* Inwardly, she cringed at that thought.

"And I've appreciated it. I know you're right. I should have told you several times, but I didn't. In the beginning it was because you were a doctor. Later it was because..." He shrugged. "I don't know. I guess I liked not having you know. I knew if and when you found out you'd hate me."

"Why shouldn't I hate you? Here I thought we were friends." *Near lovers.* "Now I discover everything's been a lie."

"Oh, no. Not a lie." He reached out to touch her, but she stepped back.

"The only thing I lied about was my last name," he insisted, watching her. His eyes were dark and searching.

Searching for what? she wondered. Understanding? Well, she didn't understand. "You said you have no job. You must be syndicated in half the newspapers across the country."

"What you're seeing now are old strips. They're reprinting them. Haven't you noticed, Leo's back to spouting innocent, nonoffensive, philosophical garbage?"

"Maybe you think it's garbage. I don't."

"You, and most of my readers," he agreed bitterly. "Three months ago my agent took me out to lunch. Brian has been my best friend for years, and he didn't mince words. Basically he said a good cartoon didn't become a personal vendetta, that Leo wasn't funny anymore, that I was alienating the medical profession and losing readers. That in turn means papers don't want me. Also the studio in California that was going to do a Saturday cartoon show of *Lyon's Pride* has put the project on hold. It *will* be produced if I go back to the old-style Leo. If not . . . Brian said it was my decision. So, I decided to walk."

"Just like that." She snapped her fingers.

He nodded and snapped his. "Just like that."

"A walk from New York to California. Why?"

"To give me time to think." As long as he was being honest, he might as well tell her everything. "At first I just wanted to get away from New York, smell the flowers as Brian had suggested. After a while, I decided it would be a good opportunity to talk to a cross section of people, hear what others thought about doctors. You'd be surprised at the stories I've been told of medical malpractice."

Amy cringed, thinking of the stories he'd gathered while at the banquet. "And when you reach California?"

"It depends on how I feel. Brian's hoping a few months off and I'll be ready to go back to the old style of *Lyon's Pride*. I'm thinking I'll write a book about my experiences." He half-smiled. "If I illustrate it with pictures of Leo, some people might buy it."

"A book about walking across America or about incompetent doctors?"

He didn't answer, and she knew. "Why do you hate doctors so much?"

"Because doctors took away my childhood."

"I don't understand."

She was afraid he wouldn't tell her. Turning away, he moved to the windows and stared out. A robin landed on the grass, hopping about, looking for worms. Amy doubted Greg even saw it. His thoughts were focused inward. Finally, he spoke. "My mother was a sick woman. She was always telling people she was, but her illness extended beyond her hypochondria. In her mind, I was her possession, a possession she wouldn't let out of her sight."

"A possession?" Amy moved closer.

He glanced her way, then back out the window. His body was tense, his hands clenched in fists. "One doctor told me that somewhere back in her childhood, she'd missed out on getting the love and attention she needed, that the reason she did what she did was she was looking for love and attention. He made her behavior sound reasonable. Gave reasons for everything.''

Greg swung around on his crutches so he was facing her. ''What she did was not reasonable.''

His were the eyes of a man ready to do battle. Amy didn't want to fight with him. She wanted to understand. ''Tell me about your mother.''

''From pictures I've seen, she was beautiful when she was young. Blond. Blue-eyed. I can see why my father married her. I also understand why he left her, but it took me years before I knew about that.'' He paused. ''I guess I should tell you the whole story.''

''Please.''

''Well, I really don't remember much about my father, other than he was tall and thin and used to yell a lot, especially whenever I got an asthma attack.''

''You have asthma,'' she interrupted. She'd never seen any signs of it.

''Had,'' he corrected. ''As a child. Or at least I'm pretty sure I had it. I do remember being afraid to go to sleep because I'd wake up unable to breathe. That's when the sleeping pills started.''

''Sleeping pills? When you were a child?'' It didn't make sense.

''My mother said I had to go to sleep, otherwise I'd upset my father. So she'd give me a pill, and I'd sleep.'' He rolled his eyes upward. ''And sleep.''

''What did your father do if you got an asthma attack?''

''Yell at me. He was always yelling at me, telling me I was just like my mother. He scared me. I was only four when my mother told me my father had left us, that he was dead, and that we had to stick together. I really thought he was dead. It wasn't until I was eighteen that I found out my father had deserted us, walked out on her and on me.''

Greg looked outside again. "I still remember the day the lawyer stopped by to say my father had recently died and left me some money. I told him my father had died fourteen years before. It took a legal death certificate before I saw the truth. For fourteen years my mother had lied to me. It blew my mind."

Amy tried to imagine what it had been like for him, the surprise and confusion. She could tell it still bothered him.

"I guess I can understand why he left me with her. I was small for my age. Thin. Always getting those asthma attacks. Why take a kid with you if he's sickly?"

Amy ached for the boy she saw in the man, the child who really didn't understand.

"It seemed natural when I turned five for my mother to decide I was too ill to go to school, that I needed to be home-schooled. She did it all very legal and right, brought in special teachers. And if a teacher ever said anything about my always being tired, she'd be replaced. They came and they went, one face blending into another."

"Why were you always tired?"

"Because my mother kept giving me pills."

"What kinds of pills?"

"Antihistamines, tranquilizers, sedatives, barbiturates. You name it."

"How'd she get them?" Most of what he'd named required a prescription to be obtained.

His smile was sardonic. "From doctors. Wonderful, money-hungry, pill-pushing doctors who didn't give a damn about anything except getting another patient into their offices and more money for their pleasures."

"Doctors prescribed tranquilizers and barbiturates for you?"

"Mostly the antihistamines for me, the tranquilizers and sedatives for her. But I'd end up with them. 'Medication for your asthma,' she'd tell me and force me to take them. I was so doped up, I rarely had the energy to go out of the house. Had no friends my age. I was hers. Maybe I was in a stupor, but I would never leave her."

"Didn't the doctors get wise to her after a while?"

"If they did, they didn't care. And she was seeing a slew of doctors. She'd get something different from each. Tranquilizers from one. A sedative from another. She loved going to doctors. You name the disease, and she was sure she had it. Another way of getting attention, the psychiatrists said."

"When did you see a psychiatrist?"

"While I was in the army. I was so angry with my mother lying about my father, I took off from the apartment and decided to join the army." He laughed. "Actually, it was a gesture of defiance. I didn't really think the army would take me. Not with my asthma. I just wanted to scare her with the idea that I'd signed up and could leave if I wanted. What a surprise when they said I'd passed my physical, that there were no signs of asthma, and that I was a perfectly healthy eighteen-year-old.

"Everything I'd been led to believe as a child was falling apart. My father hadn't died when I was four, and I wasn't sickly. When I tried talking to my mother, she started clinging to me and crying. She told me I was a stupid fool for enlisting, begged me not to leave her, then threatened to stop me. I reacted by going ahead and going into the army. I figured I'd show her, that I'd make her suffer." Again he chuckled. "I was the one who did a lot of suffering."

"I imagine boot camp must have been quite a shock to you."

"It almost did me in. Simply mixing with a platoon of men was a shock. Remember, I'd spent all of my life in the solitude of an apartment or with just my home teachers and a few select friends. Army life was hell, but in some ways it was also a wonderful experience—for the first time in my eighteen years, I was off all medication. I still felt tired all the time, but this was a different tiredness, an exhaustion from putting in a full day of work. And I could tell I was getting stronger.''

She wasn't sure if he realized he was doing it, but he flexed his arm muscles, and she remembered how strong those arms had felt whenever he held her close. Kissed her.

Quickly she shook off the memory. That was another time. Another person. ''You never had any asthma attacks while you were in the army?''

''None. Nor any since. Actually, I don't remember having an attack from around the age of six on. My mother always said I didn't because of the medication she had me on. The army doctor said I probably outgrew it.''

''Have you been checked for liver damage? Bone or nerve damage?'' She hated to think of what the medication he'd been on might have done to his internal organs.

''Yes. No signs of any problems. One thing I must say, my mother was careful. She kept switching drugs. Kept the dosage low. Just enough to keep her son docile. Keep me at her side.''

''She never took you to a doctor?''

''Oh, I was into the doctor's for everything. I'd sneeze and I saw a doctor. Run a fever and I was in the emergency room.''

''I can't believe no doctor realized what she was doing to you.''

Greg grinned smugly. ''My point, exactly. Why didn't they? And why was a woman whom they had to know was psychotic and drinking heavily given drugs which, when mixed with alcohol, would kill her? It's the doctors I blame. For her death and my loss of a childhood.''

Finally she did understand. ''So you've condemned us all and lashed out through Leo.''

''And ended up living with a doctor. Ironic, isn't it?''

"And how will I appear in your book, Greg? The foolish doctor who thought she could change your mind and ended up merely giving you more horror stories?" She wished she'd never taken him to that banquet.

"No. Being around you has made me question some of my ideas."

"And, of course, you've now changed your mind about the entire medical profession." She knew he hadn't.

He stared at her face, then shook his head. "I care the world for you, honey, but I haven't changed my mind about the medical profession as a whole. The people I talked to during the first forty-seven days of my cross-country walk all had horror stories to tell about doctors. I imagine I'll hear more."

"Well, you're going to have a chance to hear them soon. When I get back from making calls this afternoon, I want you out of my house."

She thought he would argue with her. He merely nodded. When she left, he was in his room packing. She didn't say goodbye, she couldn't. She wanted to forget he'd ever existed.

But before she was a mile down the road, she knew she couldn't send him off like that, couldn't pretend he'd never touched her, kissed her. She had scars. Well, he had open wounds, and she was a doctor.

When she came back to the house and limped through the doorway to his room, his backpack was zipped closed and he was leaving several hundred-dollar bills on the dresser.

"Forget the money. You're going to pay me in another way."

Surprised, he turned to face her. "What way's that?"

"You and I are going on the Opal Robinson show together. You want me to be on display? All right, fine. I'll get in front of a camera and let people see what I look like. But you're going to be sitting next to me. And you're going to tell people what's making you so damned angry."

"I will not be coerced into anything," he insisted.

"Who's coercing you? I'm giving you the opportunity of a lifetime. You can berate doctors all you want. On national television. And I'm going to defend my profession. For over a year you've been able to make your snide comments without anyone able to come back with a rebuttal. Well, I think you owe me that opportunity."

"The idea of going on that show was to get money for your clinic. For an X-ray machine."

"Maybe I think this is more important." That *he* was more important.

"You're crazy."

"Probably." She turned to leave. "Call and get us on that show. I'll be back in a few hours."

"And how do you know I'll be here when you get back?"

She hesitated only a moment, then looked back and smiled. "You'll be here because Leo wouldn't run away from a fight. Because I pulled a thorn from his paw and now he owes me."

"You're confusing Leo with Androcles."

"No. I'm Androcles, and you owe me, Greg." Her gaze moved to the money on the dresser then back to his face. "And I don't want your money."

Amy thought the afternoon would never end. She prayed she'd judged rightly, that Greg would be at the house when she returned. Peggy was the first person she saw. The older woman looked worried. "He told me who he is," she said. "And what you want to do. Do you think that's wise?"

"Yes." The word sounded stronger than she felt. "Someone needs to defend the medical profession against what he's been saying."

"And you think you can do it?" Peggy's eyes narrowed questioningly. "Feelin' as you do about him?"

"What I feel right now is anger. He deceived me. Deceived all of us."

"And she's going to put me in my place," Greg said and swung his crutches into the kitchen.

Amy couldn't believe the change in him. He'd shaved off his beard and moustache. His cheeks and chin were pale and tinged pink, giving him a younger, more boyish appearance. He stopped in the doorway and looked her over, from the top of her head to the toes of her walking shoes. To her dismay, Amy felt goose bumps rise on her skin.

Her body was undermining her resolve to stay angry, but she'd be damned if she'd let him know. "Did you get us on?"

"You haven't changed your mind?" he asked.

"No, I haven't changed my mind."

"Okay, then I'll call."

From the moment Greg made that call and explained the situation, things happened quickly. Within a week, dozens of phone calls took place between Wyngate, Indiana, and Chicago, Illinois. Having G. M. Lyon agree to an on-camera debate with a small-town Indiana doctor, that was news.

Seven days after Amy learned Greg's true identity, he had a walking cast on his right leg and they were on their way to Chicago. Everything was being rushed. The show would be aired the day after it was filmed. Greg had insisted on that. She knew he wanted to get it over with and leave. Their relationship had turned from their being near-lovers to barely speaking.

At nine in the morning, a limousine picked them up in front of the clinic and drove them to the airport in Indianapolis. From there they were flown to Chicago. Peggy came along. It seemed appropriate since she was so much a part of Amy's relationship with Greg. Amy's mother, father, and sister would join them for the taping.

Greg invited Brian. Brian didn't like the idea of Greg going on the show, but said he'd be there.

That night they stayed at one of Chicago's finest hotels, in separate rooms, and ate—compliments of the show—at the hotel's restaurant. Although they'd traveled together and arrived together, the strained distance between Greg and Amy continued. He sat at one table, by himself. She sat with Peggy. Peggy had never been to Chicago or to a hotel or a fancy restaurant. Peggy savored every bite of her food, marveled at the decor and watched everyone who came and went.

Peggy was having a marvelous time; Amy was miserable.

As Peggy talked on, incessantly, Amy tried to listen, tried to eat her food and tried to pretend she was unaware of Greg's presence. Only she knew exactly how long the waitress lingered at his table, talking to him. And she knew exactly when he got up to leave. Her heart stopped beating when he paused at their table. For a moment he simply stared at her, and she stared at him, wanting to say something but not knowing what to say. Then he nodded at Peggy and said good-night.

After dinner, Amy went directly to bed. Not that she could sleep. Thousands of questions bothered her. Was she doing the right thing? Would it help Greg to talk about what had happened? Could she defend her profession?

The one thing she didn't worry about was her scars. With Greg on the show, who would be looking at her?

The next morning, she was sure everyone would notice her. Her hair looked like straw in the wind, she couldn't find her lipstick and her makeup did nothing to hide her scars.

Another limousine took them to the studio, and they were whisked in through the side door. A producer came over to chat, giving them a summary of how Opal planned to introduce them. Greg said something to the man, and minutes later Amy found herself in a small room. A smiling, bubbly woman near forty came in, introduced herself as Donna, offered Amy a soda and proceeded to do things with a comb and a can of hair spray that Amy wouldn't have believed possible. Donna moved quickly and with the confidence of a pro. Deftly she applied makeup to Amy's face, then lipstick. When the woman was finished, Amy had to admit, "I don't look half-bad."

"Time to go on," the producer announced, sticking his head in. "Is she ready?"

"Ready and waiting," Donna answered and gave Amy a wink. "Knock 'em dead."

Chapter Thirteen

"Amy, I thought your mouth was going to hit the floor when Opal asked Greg if staying at your house wasn't like sleeping with the enemy." Her sister laughed and glanced across the restaurant at the table where Greg sat with a tall, lanky, good-looking middle-aged man.

"His answer was cute," Amy's mother said. "Calling Peggy your chaperon."

It was obvious neither her mother nor Chris thought a chaperon was necessary, and Amy wished she had the nerve to tell them it was a good thing Peggy had been around or she certainly *would* have been sleeping with the enemy.

"I thought I'd die," Peggy said, "when Opal came rushing over to see if that was true, if I was their chaperon. I still don't think she believes I'm there because my house is being repaired."

Peggy looked around the table they were sharing at the restaurant. Clearly she wanted all of them to believe her. Amy's mother gave the necessary assurance. "You know how these talk-show hosts are. Always trying to make something out of nothing.''

''Exactly,'' Peggy agreed.

Amy pushed her salad around on her plate, wondering if her stomach would ever settle down. Going on national television had been bad enough, but being able to see Greg yet having him so far away was keeping her insides in a turmoil.

He'd said he needed to talk to his agent. She knew he was angry with her. If he'd thought she'd merely let him tell his story and slam doctors without an argument on her part, he'd discovered just how wrong he was.

''Listening to the two of you argue, it amazes me you are both living in the same house,'' Amy's father said.

''You did good, little sister.'' Chris gave her a thumbs-up. ''Must have been from when you helped me study for the bar exam. If you ever decide you don't want to be a doctor, you certainly could consider law.''

''All I wanted to do was correct some misinformation he was giving.'' *And change his mind.* Amy felt she'd succeeded on the first. She wasn't sure about changing his mind. He'd still been citing examples of doctors' errors when the producer signaled to cut.

''Well, I think you had the audience with you.'' Chris again glanced Greg's way. ''Too bad he's so against doctors. You two looked good together. That agent of his is kind of cute. Know if he's married or anything?''

''Chris...'' Amy groaned. ''Is your divorce even final?''

''Close enough.'' She grinned at Amy, then looked back at Greg's table.

Peggy glanced that way, too. ''It's still hard f'r me t'realize he's the one who draws *Lyon's Pride*. I just thought he was some no-account, though I've got t'admit, the guy is kinda nice. Not that I'd ever tell him that.''

"He can't be all that dead set against doctors, Amy," her father pointed out. "He's the one who made sure you got a chance to talk about your clinic and your need for a new X-ray machine."

Her mother agreed. "And look at how he's donating one of his original drawings of Leo to be auctioned off. That should bring in a nice sum."

"Peggy's right," Amy agreed. "No matter what, he's a nice guy."

She watched Greg shake his head at something his agent said. She was still staring at his profile when he turned and looked her way. They were separated by tables and people, but she could feel him reach out and touch her. His gaze slid over her face, resting for a moment on her lips, then he turned back to his friend, and she felt alone.

Two hours later, after hugs and kisses and promises that they'd be down to Wyngate for the auction, Amy's parents and sister left Amy and Peggy at O'Hare Airport. Amy knew Greg was booked on the same plane as she and Peggy were, but she hadn't seen him since they'd left the restaurant. Even by the time boarding was started, she still hadn't seen him.

"Where could he be?" Peggy fussed, stepping out of the line of passengers making their way toward the gate.

"Probably on his way back to New York City." Amy forced herself to look straight ahead. If he was gone, there was nothing she could do about it.

If...

Inside the plane, she chewed on her lower lip and stared at the back of the seat in front of her. Someone had drawn a face on the No Smoking symbol, and there were scratches on the upright tray's back. Peggy was twisting and turning in her seat, pushing her purse out of the way, lowering the

shade on the window, then positioning the pillow she'd
pulled out of the rack above so it cushioned her head.

All three seats on the opposite side of the aisle remained
empty. Greg was supposed to have the aisle seat. Amy re-
fused to look for him, but she was aware of every passenger who came down the aisle. Finally a heavyset man took
the window seat. From the corner of her eye, she watched
him settle in, then open a newspaper and begin to read.

The plane was nearly full when she heard the uneven
thump of Greg's steps. He was next to her, looking directly
at her, when she glanced up. She wasn't sure how to describe his expression. Guarded, maybe. Perhaps amused.

"'Bout time you showed up," Peggy scolded. "Whadaya think? You're so highfalutin' important they'll hold this
plane f'r you?"

"I saw Brian off." He glanced at his watch. "I did cut it
rather close."

As far as Amy could tell, he was the last passenger on. No
sooner did he sit down than the attendants began giving
their spiel on seat belts and emergency exits.

Peggy fell asleep the moment the plane was in the air.
Amy was too keyed up to relax. Greg was on the plane. He
was going back to Wyngate with them. But for how long?
And why did she even want him to stay?

The way they'd argued that morning, anyone listening to
them would have thought they were bitter enemies. Opal had
played them off each other like an expert, and the audience
had loved every minute.

Mentally Amy began to replay the entire show, starting
with the moment she was introduced. She was glad she
hadn't had to limp on stage with the cameras rolling. Greg
coming on later—looking so noble with his hair haloing his
clean-shaven face and his suit trousers just barely showing
his walking cast—had been far more effective.

A hand touched her arm, and she jumped in surprise, then looked across the aisle. "Move over here." Greg nodded toward the empty seat beside him. "We need to talk."

Maybe they'd spent an hour that morning arguing, but they hadn't talked. Not to each other. They hadn't really talked for over a week. She got up and he slid over to the empty seat in the middle so she could have the aisle seat. The man by the window glanced their way, then went back to reading his paper.

"You surprised me this morning," Greg said, a hint of respect in his tone. "My little impala has turned into a lioness."

"Impala?"

"I see people as animals. You used to remind me of an impala."

"They're small, graceful animals. I'm hardly graceful."

"So, you were an impala with a limp." He grinned.

"And you were the lion," she realized. "Ready to pounce on me. Tear me to shreds."

"It didn't work out that way, did it? I'd say you did a pretty good job of shredding some of my arguments."

"I hope so. The question is, did I change your mind about doctors?"

He hesitated a moment, then shook his head. "No."

"Then I guess I didn't do that good of a job."

"You looked good on television," he said.

"That I wouldn't know." She'd purposefully avoided looking at the screen. "If I did, I owe it to you."

"How's that?"

"For getting Donna to do my hair and makeup." She knew Greg was the one who'd suggested it. "For getting them to have me seated when the show began."

He didn't deny it. "Why not let you look your best? As you said, this was a show about what we were doing, what we believed, not how you'd survived a terrible accident."

"I also owe you a thank you for the nice words you said about what I do in Wyngate and for plugging the auction. After what I'd said to you, that surprised me."

"We simply have a difference of opinion." He touched her hand, his fingertips lightly brushing over her knuckles.

A shiver ran up her arm, and she pulled her hand away. "Greg, I'd say it's a little more than a difference of opinion."

"So, do you want me to leave?"

She didn't have to think about her answer. He might be the enemy, but he was also the man she loved. "Stay. Please. At least until the auction."

"Do you think that's wise?"

Wisdom had nothing to do with her feelings. She nodded.

The next afternoon, Peggy came in while Greg was putting a tape in the VCR. He'd been away from the house most of the day, distributing flyers, but there was no avoiding the woman now. She sat on the couch and snorted. "Recording it so you can take it with you when you leave?"

"I'm recording it for Amy."

"She's comin' back t'see it," Peggy said.

He hadn't realized that. "She's cutting her calls short?"

Peggy stiffened. "She's not neglectin' anyone. All she had t'do today was check on th' Eisners and Molly. Nothin' that couldn't wait."

Greg picked up the remote control. "I know Amy wouldn't ignore anyone who really needed to see her. I also know if she gets a call on her beeper, she'll answer it, TV show or not."

"Y're hurtin' her."

He knew that. He just didn't know what to do to make the pain go away. "I want her to realize she's not ugly. That a man can love her just the way she is."

"And do y'love her?" Peggy asked.

He'd asked himself the same question. He gave Peggy the same answer he'd given himself. "How can I love what I hate?"

"Then y'should go."

"I promised her I'd stay until the auction."

Peggy studied his face, then sighed and shook her head. "Y'should have left that first day."

Amy glanced at her watch as she pulled into her driveway. Two minutes to four. She'd made it.

Her watch said exactly four when she entered her living room. "I feel like a kid playing hooky. Is it on yet?"

"Just about," Peggy answered and patted the cushion beside her on the couch. "Come sit down."

Amy paused. Greg wasn't on the couch or seated in either chair. Fear reached inside of her, and she looked around the room, silently praying he hadn't left. She could feel her smile when she saw him back by her bookshelf. "I saw Mel Freeman today. Your being a famous cartoonist has made him the happiest man alive. Finding you by the side of the road has become his claim to fame."

Greg moved toward her. "Probably if he'd known who I was, he would have left me there."

"Naw." She tried to make her tone sound light. "Old Mel always picks up strays. Just if he'd known who you were, he probably would have made you ride in the bed of the truck."

"It's coming on," Peggy said excitedly.

Amy remained standing beside Greg. A new tension gripped her insides. "Now I get to see what kind of fool I made of myself."

Greg watched her, not the show. First she grimaced when she saw herself, wrinkling her nose, then she shrugged. After a few minutes, she glanced his way. "Actually, I don't look too bad."

For the first time, he checked the screen. As far as he was concerned, she looked great, but he always liked the way she looked. Seated by herself on the stage, wearing her pale peach dress, she also looked small and vulnerable. She'd been his impala then.

"Ah, here comes your grand entrance. Leo the Lion in the flesh."

"I'm certainly not striding in like a lion. More like peg-leg Pete or a waddling duck."

Watching the show, he was surprised by how often he looked at Amy... and she looked at him. How even as they argued about the responsibilities of being a doctor, he leaned toward her and she leaned toward him. Their words were at odds, but their body language told another story. Greg understood why Opal had asked about "sleeping with the enemy." She'd noticed.

"Oh my, look at me," Peggy groaned. "Oh dear, I look awful. Just awful."

"You look fine," Amy and Greg said in unison, then glanced at each other. Amy grinned. "You look just fine, Peggy," she repeated.

"I look like a dowdy old spinster, that's what I look like. Why didn't y'two tell me that dress looked frumpy?"

"Frumpy?" Greg suppressed a laugh. Actually, compared to the dark-colored polyester pants and plain blouses Peggy usually wore, the print dress had seemed almost cheerful.

Amy worded her answer tactfully. "I think dark colors make a person look dignified."

The camera left Peggy and returned to Opal, and Peggy leaned back. "My few moments in th' spotlight." She laughed almost childishly. "How fleetin' fame."

"'Tis better to know fame for but a moment than never at all."

"So sayeth Leo?" Amy asked.

"Actually, that's what Brian's always saying, although I do think I used it in one strip."

The hour flew by. Whenever there was a commercial, Amy and Peggy compared notes, trying to remember what came next. Amy booed and hissed Greg when he started his tirade against doctors. Peggy applauded Amy's responses. As the last of the credits rolled by, Greg pushed the stop button, and Peggy immediately took the remote from him and rewound the tape. "This I want t'see again," she said.

Greg had seen enough. He touched Amy's arm, then silently indicated they leave the room. She nodded.

If Peggy noticed their departure, she said nothing. Greg led the way into the kitchen. "Want some iced tea?" he asked, heading for the refrigerator.

"Sure." Amy watched him get the pitcher and ice cubes. She got the glasses, and he poured.

"Let's go outside where we won't be disturbed." Without waiting for her response, he started for the back door.

The moment they stepped out of the house, they were hit by the heat of the afternoon. Greg headed straight for the shade of the gazebo, and Amy followed. She could tell this wasn't going to be a casual conversation. Her insides in knots, she sank onto one bench and took a long gulp of tea.

Lingering moisture made her lips glisten, and Greg was tempted to sit next to her and taste her mouth one more time. Instead, he leaned against the opposite wall. "You did a good job yesterday. I think you'll get your money."

"I hope so."

The telephone in the house rang. Amy started to rise, but Greg stopped her. "Let Peggy get it. We need to talk."

Amy looked down at the crushed limestone that covered the ground. "Greg, I don't think I want this talk."

"Doc Amy—" Peggy yelled from the kitchen window.

"Take a message, she'll be in later," Greg shouted back.

"Making my decisions for me now?"

"Today I am."

That was what she was afraid of. Not that she wanted to talk to anyone on the phone. It was the decision he'd made for himself that scared her. She could see it in his eyes, in the way he stood, so far away. He was distancing himself from her. Leaving.

She tried to avoid the topic. "You know, I was surprised by how good I did look on television. Not that I was any stunning beauty, but I didn't look bad for a woman nearing her thirtieth birthday."

"Not bad at all." He grinned, pleased with her assessment.

"Definitely passable."

"Definitely."

"You wanted me to see that, didn't you?"

"Yes." For her to see herself as he saw her. Precious. Beautiful.

She held her right hand up in front of her face. "Funny how as a child you get an image of yourself and no matter how much you change, you hold on to that image. When I started growing, my hands seemed huge. They were way too big for the rest of me, always getting in my way. And for years—until I was in med school—I always thought I had big hands. Then one day, when I was in the operating room, the surgeon I was observing commented that I, with my small hands, could reach places many of the men would not be able to reach. It was then that I realized my hands weren't out of proportion to my body. At least, not anymore."

Greg understood what she was saying. "Ever since we met, I've been telling you that you don't look bad."

"I know." She touched her cheek, feeling the indentations. "Unlike my hands, the marks are still there."

"But they don't look bad."

"Especially with gobs of makeup covering them."

"You didn't have that much makeup on. And you have beautiful eyes. Long, thick lashes. Nice hair. A cute nose and a beautiful mouth."

He looked at each part of her face as he named it off, finally staring at her mouth. Amy set her glass of tea down on the bench and stood. Slowly she moved across the small space to stand in front of Greg. She felt him shudder when she placed her hands on his shoulders. "Kiss me," she whispered. "Please."

"Amy—" He wanted to be strong, to be able to resist and turn away. That would be the right thing to do, the noble thing to do.

"Please, kiss me," she repeated, and he groaned and gave in.

Perhaps they did not agree on everything, but theirs was not a battle of right and wrong. They were not truly enemies, simply opposites. Lion and lioness, taking occasional swipes, yet needing each other.

He wanted her more than he'd ever wanted a woman, and one kiss would never be enough. No more than one day with her had been enough. Or one week or one month. His hands moved over her back, holding her to him.

How could he leave this woman?

How could he not?

His body shaking with passion, he drew away from her. She clung to his arms and tears filled her eyes. "I love you," she said.

"I know." They were the most beautiful words a man could hear. But they weren't enough.

"Don't go."

"I can't stay."

She squeezed her eyes shut. "You promised, Greg. You promised you'd stay until the auction."

"I know," he repeated. He also knew he had to break that promise.

Chapter Fourteen

The next day it rained. A gentle, warm summer rain.

The next day Greg was gone.

The moment Amy walked in the door after making house calls, she knew. Peggy stood by the kitchen table. "He's not here," she said sharply. "I was ov'r at my house this afternoon, checkin' on th' workers. When I came back, I found that envelope . . ." She pointed to the one lying on the middle of the table. "I checked his room. Bed's made and th' bathroom's clean as a whistle. His backpack's gone, too."

Picking up the envelope, Peggy rigidly held it toward Amy. "I didn't open it."

Amy was sure Peggy hadn't. She wasn't sure she wanted to, either. Her hands clenched by her sides, she stared at the envelope.

"See what he has t'say," Peggy demanded, holding it closer. "Maybe he just had t'go somewhere f'r a while. Maybe he'll be back soon."

Maybe. Amy clung to that possibility and took the envelope.

Inside she found money. He'd left more than enough to cover his medical costs, room and board. And he'd left a cartoon strip. A new, very personal, single panel showing Leo with a cloud over his head and big raindrops coming down. The lion was running away from a lioness and a cozy cave. In the balloon, Greg had penned in, "Some lions don't know enough to come in out of the rain."

Amy agreed.

His letter was short, small cartoon-like letters carefully spaced on a sheet of typewriter paper. He thanked her for all she'd done, thanked Peggy for the meals she'd prepared and asked Amy to give her one of the hundred-dollar bills. Then he apologized for any hurt he might have caused her. The message was not what she wanted to read. Crumpling the letter, she swore.

Peggy responded with a snort. "He's gone f'r good, isn't he?"

"He's gone."

"Did you know he was goin' t'leave?"

She'd known. Slowly Amy nodded.

"You should have asked him t'stay." Peggy glared at Amy, as though it were her fault Greg had left. "That was one good man. Did y'tell him y'loved him?"

Had it been that obvious? Amy wondered. "Yes, I told him I loved him."

"Good." Peggy nodded and looked out the window. "Man's a fool if he doesn't come back."

Amy watched the raindrops fall on the empty gazebo and wondered just who was the fool, the one who'd left or the one who'd be spending the rest of her life hoping he would come back. Finally she sighed and turned away from the window. "I hope he remembered to cover his cast."

* * *

One week later, the drawing he'd promised arrived, framed and carefully packed in a box addressed to Amy. There was a note along with the picture. A message from Brian:

Sorry for the delay, but I had to get this out of where Greg had it stored, and he asked me to have it framed. You did a great job on the show. Here's hoping you talked some sense into our friend. Enclosed is my check toward your X-ray machine. Good luck with the auction and making your goal.

Amy stared at the lion cartoon and saw Greg instead. In every pen stroke, he'd drawn himself, boldness blending with hesitancy, the animal's mane curling wildly about his head, his mouth holding a smile, while his eyes penetrated deep into her soul. Without a word, she set the picture back into the box and went up to her room. It was awhile before she came back down, her eyes red-rimmed and puffy. The next day she took the picture to the general store and had Mel put it in the front window, along with a sign informing everyone that this was the picture G. M. Lyon, the creator of *Lyon's Pride*, had donated for the auction. She figured having it out of her house would keep Greg out of her thoughts, yet somehow, every day, she found herself walking or driving by the general store and glancing at the picture.

And even with Greg gone, his publicity campaign continued. Notices kept appearing in the papers, reminding people of the place, date and time of the auction. If attendance wasn't good, it wouldn't be for a lack of effort on his part.

Probably the biggest boost to the drive was their appearance on the Opal Robinson show. Amy couldn't believe it when the producer called three days after the show aired and asked where she wanted the donations they were receiving sent. About the same time, cards and letters began arriving at the house, simply addressed to Doc Amy, Wyngate, Indiana. Some held just a few dollars, while others had checks for larger amounts. Amy finally had to hire a college student, home for summer break, to record receipts, deposit the money and prepare thank-you letters for Amy to sign. The red gauge on the thermometer outside the clinic was completely filled in. There was now enough money to run the clinic for another year and a good start toward replacing the X-ray machine. If the auction was even close to successful, Amy would be staying.

That was, if the auction even took place.

Amy sometimes wondered. The closer the date came, the more everything seemed to go wrong. First the auctioneer they'd contracted, a lifelong Wyngate resident, had a heart attack. All the while Amy was trying to get him stabilized and up to Bedford for the care he'd need, she kept wondering who she'd find to replace him.

Then three days before the auction, Greg's widespread publicity campaign about the auction proved to be too informative. Two men broke into the town hall where the auction was to be held and drove off with a truckload of donated items. That someone would steal from a project that would help so many hurt Amy. She hired a security guard to watch over the remaining merchandise for the next two nights.

The final blow came the day of the auction, when the auctioneer she'd found to replace the first one called to say he was sick. She wasn't sure what she was going to do when Mel Freeman walked into her clinic. He grinned when she told him her troubles. "Heck, I kin do th' callin'," he assured her. "Used t'do it when I was a boy, back 'bout fifty, sixty years ago."

At that point, Amy was desperate. "You're hired," she said and prayed he'd know what he was doing.

The one good part of having everything go wrong was she didn't have time to think about Greg. At least she kept telling herself she didn't have time to think about him. Somehow he always seemed to creep into her thoughts, and as she stood just inside the doorway of the town hall, watching people pour in—giving their names and getting bid numbers and filling the room until there was barely space to turn around—she wondered if Greg realized what a fantastic job he'd done publicizing the event.

It didn't seem right that he was gone. She felt he should be with her, should be standing by her side, hearing the comments she was hearing. People kept talking about how many great things had been donated, about how they hadn't even known where Wyngate was until they'd read the article then seen the Opal Robinson show. He should be hearing the words of praise for his posters, the flyers and the drawing he'd donated.

The picture of Leo had been moved from the window of the general store to its place of honor on an easel by the podium where Mel would be calling the auction. Mel picked up the microphone and blew into it, the sound reverberating off the walls. Amy wondered just where Greg was at that moment. Was he camped somewhere alongside a road? Talking to someone about how terrible doctors were? Adding to his anger and bitterness?

Or was he thinking about the auction? About her?

An adjustment brought the volume down, and Mel began repeating, "Testin'. One, two, three."

The auction was about to begin, and the crowd moved away from the items displayed behind the rope barriers along the sides of the long building to sit down in the chairs set up in the middle of the room or to go over to the concession stand where Peggy's Ladies' Aide Society was selling coffee, sodas, iced tea, hot dogs and cookies. Amy knew enough to stay away from the coffee. Her stomach was already shooting acid, her body stressed to the limit. If this was something that would have to be done every year, she wasn't sure she could handle it.

"Sold!" Mel called out and slammed down his gavel. "T'number sixty-four."

The first item had been sold, and Amy felt some of the tension ease out of her shoulders. The auction had started. Now it was merely a matter of time—and money.

After an hour, she was amazed by Mel's talents. He was doing a marvelous job. Even with simple items like hand-hewn ax handles he was able to get the bidding up to far more than market value. "My dog statue brought a good price," Aaron said proudly and handed Amy a cup of iced tea.

She took the cup, though she wasn't sure her stomach was ready for iced tea, either. "It was a great carving, Aaron. Mel's getting a good price for everything. Sometimes that man amazes me."

"Sometimes you amaze me." Aaron hesitantly touched her bare arm, running a fingertip up from her elbow toward the narrow strap of her sundress. "Want to celebrate after this is over?"

She faced him and wished her feelings were different for this man. Aaron was truly a nice person. A good friend. He'd certainly been understanding when he came back from Oregon. She'd known he would know what had happened while he was gone. Wyngate's grapevine was as efficient as ever. What she hadn't been sure of was Aaron's reaction.

He'd been kind and supportive, offering a shoulder to cry on if she needed one or an ear if she wanted to talk. She'd thanked him, but she'd cried herself dry and hadn't been ready to talk about Greg. Not then.

She still wasn't ready to talk about Greg. Or to go out with anyone else. "It wouldn't be a good idea," she said. "I'll be tired. Rotten company."

"Still thinking about him?"

She nodded.

"As I told you when I came back, anytime you want to talk, just give me a call."

And what could she say? Aaron, I fell in love with a man who walked away and will never be back. "Thanks," she murmured and took a sip of her tea.

"'Course, I might not be around."

He let the idea dangle, and Amy cocked her head, waiting for him to go on.

"I'm thinking of moving to Bedford. There are more opportunities for me there."

She understood he meant more than career opportunities for a stone carver. Aaron wanted a wife. A family. His choices were limited in Wyngate. Her nod was sincere. "You've been a good friend, Aaron. I wish you happiness."

"For you, too." The tousle he gave her hair was affectionate, then he moved on, over to a section of the room where several of Wyngate's male population were gathered.

The room grew quieter when Mel walked over to the drawing on the easel. "Most of y'folks from around here know th' story behind this drawing," he related. "But f'r y'newcomers, let me tell y'bout a man I found lyin' 'longside th' road one very cold and rainy night last May."

Amy listened with the rest of the people in the building. Maybe Mel embellished the story a bit here and there, making her sound like Mother Teresa for taking Greg in, fixing his broken ankle and giving him a place to stay.

"You saw them together on the Opal Robinson show," Mel went on. "They fought like cats and dogs . . ."

More like a lion and a lioness, Amy thought, pleased with the image. Maybe her body was scarred and she walked with a limp, but like a seasoned lioness, she was proud and strong and could hold her own. She could attract a male lion if she wanted.

"He's gone on," Mel finished. "He's walkin' all th' way t'California, but he didn't forget th' town of Wyngate, and he gave us this picture—one of his early, original, ink drawings of Leo—f'r this here auction."

Mel looked out over the crowd. "Do I hear one thousand dollars?"

Amy couldn't believe he was starting so high. She'd entertained the idea of buying the drawing. As a reminder, she told herself. A symbol of what she needed to strive for. One look at that drawing would be enough to make her more careful in writing a prescription, more concerned about the health and welfare of children and more willing to look beyond the surface of anyone she met.

The first bid was five hundred dollars. Amy found that more reasonable. She was shocked when her father bid eight hundred, then later when her sister bid a thousand. Amy figured she could go to two thousand. She had that much in savings bonds put aside for a rainy day. This definitely constituted a rainy day.

The bidding slowed at fifteen hundred, and Amy signaled fifteen-fifty. Several people turned to look at her. An out-of-towner bid sixteen hundred, then another went to sixteen-fifty. Amy waited a moment before saying seventeen hundred.

Mel looked at her, then grinned. "Well, whadaya know," he murmured into the mike, then nodded. Immediately he picked up the bidding. "I have seventeen hundred. Do I hear eighteen?"

The out-of-towner gave seventeen-fifty. People looked at her then. She was sure they were waiting for her to go to eighteen. A buzz seemed to move through the hall, one person turning to the next, saying something, then that person looking her way.

Amy decided if they were that eager to see her raise the bid, she wouldn't disappoint them. "Eight—"

A hand on her shoulder stopped her. "Let someone else have it, honey," a familiar, sexy voice purred near her ear. "I'll draw you another."

"Greg!" she cried, turning into his arms.

He held her, rocking her in his embrace. No one in the room said a word, and Greg looked up at Mel. "I think she's glad to see me," he said loudly.

Laughter filled the room.

"We're all glad t'see you," Mel announced through the speakers, then slipped back into his singsong chant. "I have seventeen-fifty. Do I hear eighteen? We've got th' artist himself, right here."

"I can't believe you're here," Amy kept repeating, oblivious to everything but Greg.

He was wearing a black T-shirt, shorts and hiking shoes. His hair was as long as ever, and he'd grown back his beard. The only thing missing was his cast. "How's your ankle? Any problems?"

"Always the doctor." He chuckled. "My ankle's fine. I'm still limping a little, but I'm getting stronger every day." He held her away from himself. "You look good. Sexy."

She blushed. "It's just a cotton sundress."

"It's not the dress I'm talking about." Although the red dress with its thin straps and figure-revealing lines didn't hurt the image. "Do you have any empty bedrooms in that mansion of yours for a weary traveler?"

"I just might. Peggy's not at the house anymore."

"That's good."

"But my parents are staying with me. And my sister."

"That's bad." He lifted his eyebrows. "For how long?"

She grinned. "For just a few days."

Pleased, he nodded. "That's good."

"Sold, for three thousand five hundred!" Mel called and Amy jerked her head in his direction.

"My gosh, how'd it get that high?" she exclaimed.

"It's the magnetism of my presence," Greg insisted and steered her toward the door. "Let's get out of here."

They kissed outside the town hall, and they kissed in her car. They kissed before they went into her house and they kissed after they were in her house. It was only when her parents and sister arrived that they stopped kissing, but even then Greg kept his arm around Amy, possessively marking her as his.

Everyone had questions. He tried to answer each. "I got as far as St. Louis," he explained to all of them. "Walking on a cast didn't work, so I rented a car and made a lot of stops along the way. I asked people about their doctors and problems they'd had. I got about the same responses as before, some good, some bad. Funny thing, though, with the ones who told me about problems, I began questioning them about what they'd done or hadn't done. What was worse, I even started defending some practices."

He squeezed Amy's shoulders. "Mark Twain once said, 'Travel is fatal to prejudice, bigotry and narrow-mindedness.' He was right. Traveling to Wyngate, Indiana and meeting you was the worst thing that could have happened to me."

Amy looked up, and he grinned. "You ruined a perfectly good hate campaign."

"She can be very persuasive," her father agreed. "I remember the day she announced she was going to be a doctor. We all tried to talk her out of it. Her mother and I felt that with her leg she wouldn't be able to handle the physical requirements of the work. By the end of that afternoon,

I was filling out financial-aid papers and listening to the pros and cons of various medical schools.''

There was a knock at the back door, but before anyone could get it, Peggy walked in. Sternly, she looked Greg up and down. "See y're back."

"Like that bad penny."

"Am I gonna have t'have more work done on my house?"

Greg grinned. "Could be."

She snorted and looked at Amy. "I just stopped by t'tell you, y'did real good tonight. Real good. Mel said he'd give you a final figure tomorrow."

Peggy nodded at Amy's sister and parents, then looked back at Greg. "Tweetie missed you."

"And I missed Tweetie," he responded, smiling at her.

It was nearly eleven before Amy's parents said good-night and Chris grabbed a romance from Amy's collection in the living room and headed for a bedroom. "Want to go outside?" Greg asked, glancing toward the gazebo.

"Mosquitoes will eat us alive."

"I have my trusty, sure-to-keep-them-away mosquito repellent," he informed her and dug into his backpack.

Once they were both covered, they went out, the evening still warm and fireflies lighting the way across the lawn. Mosquitoes buzzed around Amy's head, but none landed. In the shadows of the gazebo, with the songs of the night insects and the throaty calls of frogs as a background, Greg took her into his arms. "I know we don't know each other very well."

"Sometimes you can know a person in a day," she said.

"You're a doctor. I never went to school. All I have is a high school Equivalency Diploma."

"You're not dumb, Greg. Or uneducated."

"Thank goodness for books." He blew her bangs aside and kissed her forehead. "I'm not poor, but most of my money's tied up in investments. Even if I didn't go back to doing *Lyon's Pride,* we could probably live off the interest, but I think I am going to give Leo another try. Not the old style, though. I've changed too much for that."

She understood. She'd never again be the same person she was before she'd met him.

"The way I've been thinking of Leo lately is like a watchdog." He chuckled. "Or more appropriately, a lion guarding his pride. In the strip, I'll still be taking potshots at doctors, but Leo's going to attack a few politicians, too. And insurance salesmen. And lawyers."

Amy grinned. "I'll warn my sister."

"Not the vicious lampooning I've been doing. And mostly I think Leo might just do a little philosophizing about what it's like living in the Midwest."

"Where in the Midwest?" She hoped she knew.

"Say southern Indiana?"

"Sounds good to me."

"I love you, Amy."

She wrapped her arms around his neck and rose up on her toes." I know," she said and kissed him.

* * * * *

**Three All-American beauties discover
love comes in all shapes and sizes!**

ALL-AMERICAN SWEETHEARTS

by Laurie Paige

CARA'S BELOVED (#917)—*February*
SALLY'S BEAU (#923)—*March*
VICTORIA'S CONQUEST (#933)—*April*

A lost love, a new love and a hidden one, three *All-American Sweethearts* get their men in Paradise Falls, West Virginia. Only in America... and only from Silhouette Romance!

If you missed *Cara's Beloved* or *Sally's Beau*, the first two titles in the All-American Sweethearts trilogy, please send your name, address, zip or postal code, along with a check or money order (do not send cash) for $2.69 for each book ordered, plus 75¢ postage and handling ($1.00 in Canada), payable to Silhouette Books, to:

In the U.S.	In Canada
Silhouette Books	Silhouette Books
3010 Walden Avenue	P.O. Box 609
P.O. Box 1396	Fort Erie, Ontario
Buffalo, NY 14269-1396	L2A 5X3

Please specify book title(s) with your order.
Canadian residents add applicable federal and provincial taxes.

SRLP3

Silhouette
R O M A N C E™

INTIMATE MOMENTS®
10TH
Anniversary

Celebrate our anniversary with a fabulous collection of firsts....

The first Intimate Moments titles written by three of your favorite authors:

NIGHT MOVES Heather Graham Pozzessere
LADY OF THE NIGHT Emilie Richards
A STRANGER'S SMILE Kathleen Korbel

Silhouette Intimate Moments is proud to present a FREE hardbound collection of our authors' firsts—titles that you will treasure in the years to come from some of the line's founding members.

This collection will not be sold in retail stores and is available only through this exclusive offer. Look for details in Silhouette Intimate Moments titles available in retail stores in May, June and July.

SIMANN

A romantic collection that
will touch your heart....

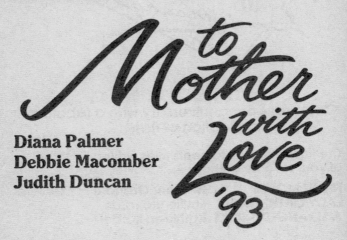

_to_
Mother
with
Love
'93

Diana Palmer
Debbie Macomber
Judith Duncan

As part of your annual tribute to
motherhood, join three of Silhouette's
best-loved authors as they celebrate the
joy of one of our most precious gifts—
mothers.

Available in May at your favorite retail outlet.

Only from 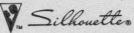 _Silhouette_®

—where passion lives.

SMD93

Silhouette Books
is proud to present
our best authors,
their best books...
and the best in
your reading pleasure!

Throughout 1993, look for exciting books
by these top names in contemporary
romance:

CATHERINE COULTER—
Aftershocks in February

FERN MICHAELS—
Nightstar in March

DIANA PALMER—
Heather's Song in March

ELIZABETH LOWELL
Love Song for a Raven in April

SANDRA BROWN
(previously published under
the pseudonym Erin St. Claire)—
Led Astray in April

LINDA HOWARD—
All That Glitters in May

When it comes to passion,
we wrote the book.

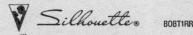

BOBT1RR